FRIENDS LIST

By Rob Watson

FRIENDS LIST

Limitless Publishing, LLC
Kailua, HI 96734
www.limitlesspublishing.com

Formatting: Limitless Publishing

ISBN-13: 978-1-64034-284-2
ISBN-10: 1-64034-284-2

DEDICATION

For Robert Randolph Watson, Sr. Everything and anything that is good in me, I owe to you. I shall spend my life trying to live up to your name—your name, which I am greatly honored to share. I love you, Dad.

CHAPTER ONE

ROOMMATES

Kimberly Clark sat in front of her laptop computer wearing only knee-high athletic socks and a California State University, Long Beach long-sleeved sweatshirt. Her shoulder-length, strawberry blonde hair alluringly framed her heart-shaped face that housed a dazzling pair of emerald green eyes. She yawned, her black-painted fingernails navigating to the homepage of the Roommates website, an online virtual community whose members created their own virtual rooms where their friends, or mates, may visit, leave text messages, or IM chat.

Her off-campus apartment was dark. The only source of illumination, the light from her laptop, eerily reflected off of Kimberly in such a way that her makeup-less face appeared cold and lifeless. Posters of alternative rock bands and modelesque young men adorned the walls, and cute stuffed animals lined the shelves, as one would expect to

1

find in a young woman's "I'm no longer a child, but don't wanna be an adult yet" apartment.

Although it was a safe neighborhood, the front door was locked because of recent reports of prowlers in the area. Wary from these reports, Kimberly was considering signing up for the women's self-defense class at the university.

I'll check it out, she thought. *Maybe after my abnormal psych final. Maybe.*

On her laptop screen, Kimberly moved the pointer to the "MEMBERS" icon and clicked her mouse's button. The homepage changed to the login screen with the message:

Welcome to Roommates. To enter your room, please type your username and password.

Kimberly typed in the information and then hit the Enter key. The laptop screen dissolved to a screen with a picture of a door with a name plate that read:

Kimber's Room.

The door opened and the screen dissolved into the graphical representation of a young woman's bedroom. A busty avatar representing Kimberly appeared and winked. The virtual bedroom contained many icons and links, and an address book on the desk graphic. The address book listed Kimberly's best friends, or "Mates," in numerical order, with Lexa Rhodes topping the list.

FRIENDS LIST

Kimberly moved the cursor to the jukebox graphic and selected track number twenty-two. Her avatar walked over to the jukebox graphic, pressed a button, and danced about as dark and brooding alternative rock music blasted through her laptop's speakers.

She moved her mouse and clicked another icon, and a pop-up window appeared on screen:

Kimber's Blog.

Kimberly typed:

Going to Catalina for a week or so. Looking forward to putting some distance between me and my soon-to-be-ex-boyfriend. Or, as Lexa calls him, The Fuckwad. Maybe this will give me the time and space (and opportunity) I need to work through a dilemma I'm facing.

Kimberly let out a deep, wanton sigh after catching sight of a framed picture sitting off to the side of her desk. The photograph was of herself posing seductively with her best friend Lexa Rhodes, a sexy, dark-haired young woman of twenty-two.

Kimberly's glance became a long, lustful stare. She moistened her rose pink lips with her tongue as she studied every feature of Lexa's toned, nubile body. Her thoughts confused her.

I've never been a lesbian, or even bi-sexual. And

even if I was, it would be so wrong to try and get with my BFF. My straight BFF at that.

Kimberly's lusty gaze caressed the photographed image of her friend.

But every time I see Lexa, or just even think about her—ooooh my god!

As Kimberly gazed longingly at the photo, Lexa and herself came to life inside the picture, turned toward each other, and kissed passionately. Like frothy ocean waves erasing hand-drawn words in the sand, her reservations for lusting after her best friend were quickly washed away by the wetness building between her thighs.

She rubbed her finger across her wet lips, and then down over her hardened nipples. Just as she moved her hand down between her thighs, the telephone rang. Kimberly sighed and turned down the music's volume without breaking her gaze at the photograph.

The answering machine picked up the call. *"Hi, this is Kimber, you know what to do."* After the answering machine beeped, a wave of party noises jolted Kimberly out of her erotic daze and she picked up the phone.

"Hey, where are you?" asked Paige, Kimberly's outgoing, charismatic classmate and coworker.

Kimberly frowned. "Look, Paige, I already said—"

"I know what you already said, but I decided not to listen," Paige interrupted in a voice that barely audible above the background noise. *"I decided to take it upon myself to make sure your precious youth isn't prematurely wasted by missing*

yet another sick rave. Besides, I can't dance with all these gorgeous guys by myself. Not all at the same time anyway. So hurry up and get your sweet little derrière down here, okay?"

After Paige abruptly hung up, Kimberly put down her phone, picked up a pencil, and opened the notebook lying next to her laptop. She wrote "KIMBER + LEXA" on the inside cover, turned the music back up, and then turned her attention back to her blog. She let out a desperate sigh as her head battled with her heart.

Do I take a chance and tell her how I feel? she typed.

The music's volume lowered and knocking echoed through the speakers. The words ***"Someone's Knocking"*** appeared next to the door graphic. Kimberly closed her blog window and moved her avatar to the peephole.

Another dialogue box appeared, inside which Kimberly typed:

Who's there?

The peephole widened and an avatar of a hooded figure appeared. A dialogue box popped up next to the avatar, and inside the box appeared the screen name IWNTUDED.

Kimberly typed:

Do I know you?

IWNTUDED responded:

Yes. But not the way u think u do.

"Seriously, this is so not the time for this," Kimberly muttered to herself. She typed:

Doug, is that you? Look, I know you still love me, but it's over. It's nothing you did, it's just that I'm going through so many changes right now. She sighed. *I'm sorry. Tell you what. I'll give you a weekend of goodbye sex when I get back, okay?*

After a few uncomfortable moments passed, IWNTUDED responded:

Sounds like fun, but I'm not Doug.

"What the hell?" Kimberly whispered as the ambient light from the laptop's screen eerily illuminated her pretty face. She stared at the screen and typed:

Who is this?

There was a long moment before IWNTUDED responded:

The last person you'll ever see.

"Okay, fuck this," Kimberly blurted. She clicked the "KEEP OUT" icon next to Iwntuded's screen name, and the "LOCK DOOR" icon on the keyhole graphic.

"So long, creep." She picked up the Starbucks cup sitting on her Abnormal Psychology textbook, took a sip, spun her chair around, and reclined with her back to the computer.

While she sat there thinking how much easier life would be if it was this simple to get rid of people in the real world, the word "Unlock" appeared on the door graphic, and the Iwntuded avatar entered the room and approached the Kimber avatar.

Finished musing over the inherent advantages of Cybering, Kimberly turned back toward the laptop screen and was dumbstruck when she saw Iwntuded's avatar standing next to hers.

"What the hell?" She placed her Starbucks cup on the desk and then typed:

How did you get in here?

The Iwntuded avatar held up a key graphic, and then IWNTUDED typed:

I have a key.

Kimberly's heart skipped a beat. She sank down in her chair and wrapped her arms tightly around herself.

Should I be scared of this creep? She shook her head. *Of course not, this is just some acne-covered kid with nothing better to do on Datenight USA, or some overweight, balding pervert who gets off on scaring the shit out of young girls.*

Her fear morphed to anger and she sat up straight in her chair.

She typed,

Look, jerkoff, the Roommates website recorded your IP address when you logged on. So get out of here and leave me the fuck alone before I report your perverted ass.

IWNTUDED replied:

Okay. But first, will u do me a favor?

Kimberly typed:

What?

May I have a sip of that coffee?

What the fuck?

Kimberly typed:

What coffee?

After a few tension-filled moments,

IWNTUDED replied:

The Starbucks next to your keyboard.

The words on her laptop screen leapt out at Kimberly as if they were in 3D. She glanced at the Starbucks cup, after which she jumped to her feet and scanned nervously about her dimly lit apartment.

Oh my God—someone's here! But how did he get in? And where is he now—watching me?

Just as she reached for the phone to dial 911, Kimberly spotted the webcam atop her computer's monitor and a wave of relief washed over her. "You little hacker."

She sat back down and yanked the USB cable from the webcam. "Show's over, jerk wad." She smirked at her laptop screen and held her middle finger up to Iwntuded's avatar.

That wasn't very nice.

Kimberly replied:

What—ending your little peep show?

IWNTUDED typed:

No, giving me the finger.

Kimberly jumped to her feet. She glanced wildly

around the room and then back at the monitor. Fight or flight mode started setting in as she typed:

Who are u and what the fuck do u want?

I told u—I'm the last person you'll ever see. As for what I want...

On the opposite side of the unlit apartment, a closet door quietly opened. A hooded figure emerged holding a smartphone in one hand and a sixteen-inch hunting knife in the other. While Kimberly sat staring at her computer screen, the hooded figure typed on the smartphone's keypad, and the reply displayed on Kimberly's laptop screen:

It's all in my name. What's my name, Kimberly?

Wide-eyed, her hands trembling, Kimberly typed:

IWNTUDED.

IWNTUDED instantly replied:

That's what I want!

Kimberly studied her tormentor's username with the urgency her situation demanded. Then, in a dread-filled whisper, she read aloud, "I…want…you…dead."

Her eyes widened when she saw the hooded figure's reflection on her screen. Before she could turn around, the hooded figure plunged the hunting knife into her throat.

Arterial spray splashed the monitor as the figure violently thrusted the blade in and out of Kimberly's neck. Her life force gradually faded to black.

The hooded figure moved a couple of paces back, using the smartphone to take pictures of the bloody remains.

***

The hooded figure sat in a filthy, unlit room typing on the keyboard of an old and dusty desktop computer that had the appearance of something Dr. Frankenstein would have fashioned together in his laboratory. Upon a rickety, worm-ridden desk was an old CRT monitor. Displayed on the flickering screen was Lexa's Roommates page, specifically, the Friends List section where members ranked their friends, or Best Mates, in chronological order.

The hooded figure plugged a USB cable from the smartphone into the tower. On the CRT screen, a skull-shaped cursor moved to Kimberly's picture, the one occupying the number one spot on the list. Gnarled and dirty fingers typed on the keyboard, and the word "UPLOAD" appeared on-screen. The cursor moved over Kimberly's picture, and with one click of the mouse, it was replaced with a picture of her severed head laying in the lap of her mutilated corpse.

CHAPTER TWO

LEXA AND ALEX

Lexa Rhodes, a comely dark-haired twenty-two year old, sat in front of her meticulously organized dresser thinking of exotic, faraway places. With haunted green eyes, she gazed at her reversed image in an antique silver hand mirror. As she brushed her long brunette hair, she fell into a solemnly pensive state of mind.

Who is the person staring back at me from behind this reflective glass? Is she the same person that's staring into it? Will I ever figure out the answer? And if I do, will I like what I've learned?

***

Amanda Rhodes, a slender woman in her mid-fifties, cut into the neck of a large goose on a cutting board in front of her. She set the butcher's knife down on the kitchen island's quartz countertop. Her 1980s pantsuit and feathered hair

13

made her seem out of place in her modern kitchen with its stainless steel appliances and subway tile backsplash.

"Lexa, hurry or you'll be late!" she yelled, wondering whether or not she'd made the right decision.

***

Her aunt calling her name pulled Lexa back into the dreary existence she called reality. She stopped brushing her hair and gazed deep into her hand mirror.

Here we go.

She took one last glimpse of herself before placing her brush and mirror upon her dresser. When she stood up, her hand mirror slid off the brush and crashed to the floor. Expletives echoed throughout her mind at the thought of damaging one of the few things she owned that once belonged to her real mother. Lexa bent down and picked up the mirror. As she beheld her mirror image, a rogue tear trickled down her face at the sight of a jagged crack bisecting her reflection.

***

Lexa carried a small piece of luggage down the staircase. When she reached the bottom, she pasted on a smile then headed into the living room. It was a warm, inviting space whose perfectly placed furniture and immaculate appearance gave it the impression of a model home. Next to the continuously burning fireplace was a small table with two chairs. Upon the table sat an antique chessboard with large hand-carved pieces. Lexa walked up to the table. After staring at the board for a lasting moment, she moved her bishop and grinned.

"Let's see you get yourself out of that, Alex," she said while skipping toward the kitchen.

***

Amanda slammed the knife down on the cutting board in bitter defeat. "Dammit!"

"I thought proper Christians weren't supposed to swear," Lexa taunted, stepping into the kitchen and setting her carry-on bag on the kitchen table. The scent of her perfume filled the room as she sauntered over to the island. Lexa winked at her aunt, picked up the knife, and began sawing across the goose's neck.

Amanda had a dozen things she wished to say to her niece this morning, but the only thing she could force out of her mouth was, "Nervous?"

"Not nervous, just a little sad," Lexa said.

Amanda put her hand on Lexa's shoulder. "You're going to be fine without Alex, you'll see."

"Yeah..." Lexa said doubtfully. She stopped cutting on the goose and put the knife down on the island.

"Dr. Cross said it will be good for the both of you to spend some time away from each other," Amanda reminded her, trying to convince herself as well as her niece.

"Isn't it enough that we go to separate colleges? Why do we have to spend Thanksgiving away from each other too?" Lexa wrapped her arms around herself and stared down at the knife. "We've never spent a holiday apart."

Amanda picked up the knife and handed it to Lexa. "Well maybe it's about time you cut the cord and try life without Alex for a while."

Lexa cracked half a grin and approached the cutting board.

"Besides, you'll have the rest of your friends to keep you company this weekend. What is it that you call yourselves again?"

"The Mag Seven, short for the Magnificent Seven," Lexa said. She resumed cutting the goose.

***

Alex Rhodes, Lexa's twin brother, entered the living room and walked eagerly over to the chess table.

Let's see what she's left for me this time.

He examined the chessboard and smiled a "Cheshire Cat" smile.

I see you're starting to come around to my way of thinking.

***

Amanda glanced at her watch and sighed. "Where's your uncle?" she asked.

16

"He's in the garage loading the luggage," Lexa responded.

Seconds later, Alex stealthily entered the kitchen and snuck up behind his unsuspecting sister. He moved his mouth up next to her ear and whispered, "You mean Alex was loading the luggage while your uncle was complaining about his fucking back, as usual."

Lexa gave her brother a sisterly air of disapproval. "Really, Alex?" she whispered, "That was so uncalled for."

"But accurate," Alex whispered back.

"Oh, I hope we didn't forget anything," said Amanda, checking her checklist on the kitchen chalkboard.

Alex leaned forward, winked at Lexa, and headed toward the kitchen table. "You're all set, except for this." He picked up his sister's carry-on bag and tried to spin it on his finger like a basketball.

"Do you have your headache pills?" Amanda asked, her worry evident despite her attempt to conceal it.

Lexa patted the purse hanging over her shoulder. "Right here."

"What about your uncle's sea-sick pills? Do you have those?"

Lexa grinned. "You mean the ones you haven't given me yet?"

Alex grinned and shook his head.

Amanda chuckled. "I'll get them." She brushed by Alex and exited the kitchen.

Alex danced up to Lexa and bowed. "Bishop to

queen four, huh? I'll find a way out of your trap by the time you get back," he said with a smug grin.

Lexa gave her brother a condescending pat on his arm. "I doubt it."

Alex turned his smile into an exaggerated frown.

"Awww…" She hugged her sulking brother and went back to sawing on the goose.

"I don't suppose you could fit me into one of your suitcases?" asked Alex.

Lexa hesitated for a split second. "You're going to be fine without me, you'll see."

"Yeah, sure."

Lexa cut harder on the goose's neck, but still wasn't even halfway through.

"Can I at least ride with you to the landing?" Alex asked. The despair in his voice caused Lexa's eyes to water.

"Sure." Lexa squeezed her eyelids to fight back her tears.

After a few moments of awkward silence passed, Claude Rhodes, a tall, handsome man in his late fifties, opened the door to the kitchen's garage entrance and stuck in his head. "Come on or you'll miss your boat," he urged.

"Coming, Uncle Claude," Lexa said.

After Claude ducked back out of the kitchen, Alex took the knife from Lexa's hand and without a second thought chopped off the goose's head with one swift blow. "Never start what you can't finish." He laid down the knife and headed for the garage.

Lexa picked up her carry-on and followed after her brother.

CHAPTER THREE

NEVER SAY GOODBYE

Claude drove his car past several curbside check-in attendants and parked in the loading zone of the Catalina Landing, got out of the car, and opened the trunk.

Lexa peered out her window and saw her friends waiting on the sidewalk.

Paige Turner, a gorgeous blonde with green eyes and a curvaceous figure, walked up and opened Lexa's door. "I see you still like to make an entrance," Paige said in a voice so smooth and sultry that even the Pope would blush upon hearing it. "C'mon, we don't want to miss the boat, do we?"

Lexa hopped out of the car, with Alex following closely behind.

As Lexa and Alex were led away by Paige, Bastian Shadwell, a short blond with an athletic build and supporting actor looks, went over to help Claude unload the luggage.

"Let me help you with that, Mr. Rhodes,"

Bastian said in a tone so obsequious he had to strain to keep a straight face.

Claude was genuinely moved, completely missing the young man's jocular cue. "Why thank you, Sebastian."

"No problem." Bastian picked up the smallest piece of luggage and set it next to the curb. His folded arms and shit-eating grin more than made clear that his assistance had ended.

Claude shook his head and unloaded the rest of the luggage while mumbling to himself.

A bus pulled to a stop and opened its doors. Cassie Lovette, a short brunette with a dark complexion, stood in the doorway holding onto the arm of Christopher Kane, aka CK, a tall, dark-haired, handsome man in his early twenties. Cassie moved her white cane left and right as they exited the bus and approached Lexa and Paige.

"I thought Kimber was coming with you," CK said to Lexa.

"Yeah, I know," Lexa said. "Kimmy was supposed to call if she needed a ride, but she—" The chime of Lexa's smartphone interrupted her. She took it out of her purse and read its screen.

KIMBERLY: Hey Lexa. I can't make the trip with you guys but no worries. I promise I'll show up for dinner tonight.

"Kimmy's not coming till later," said Lexa, putting the phone back into her purse.

"Seriously?" Paige said with an air of selfish contempt.

"Is she okay?" asked Cassie.

"She won't be if she doesn't show," Paige snapped.

"No worries. She promised she'd make it for dinner" Lexa said. Little did she know, however, that the doubtful expression on her face was in direct conflict with the confidence in her voice, though she had no reason to anticipate her roommate's absence.

"She better. Storm's expecting all of us," CK said.

"She'll turn up," Lexa assured. "She will, I promise."

While Claude and Bastian attempted to get the attention of an attendant, Palmer Randolph, a well-groomed, attractive man in his early twenties, stepped out of a stretch limousine. He walked to the rear of the limo and held up a fifty-dollar bill.

Several attendants rushed to the limo and started checking his luggage. Bastian rolled his eyes when Palmer took out another fifty and motioned toward the Rhodes' car. Two attendants rushed over and unloaded Lexa's bags.

"Spoiled little shit," Bastian muttered under his breath.

While the attendants carried the luggage into the landing, Claude walked up to his niece and gave her a hug. "Are you sure you're up to this?" Before Lexa could reply, he went on, "Maybe you shouldn't…"

Lexa put her finger up to Claude's mouth and shushed him. "Don't worry, I'll be fine," Lexa told her uncle. The expression on her face concealed the doubt in her head as to the validity of the words she spoke.

"Of course you will," Claude said with an almost prayer-like inflection. "Bye, sweetheart. Be safe, and be well."

Lexa glanced over at her somber-looking brother standing off to the side all by himself. A twinge of pain erupted in her brain. "I will," she said. She kissed her uncle on his cheek and glanced over to the rest of the Mag Seven huddling together waiting for her to join them.

"I'll be back before you know it," she said in an attempt to reassure her worried uncle.

CK ran up to Claude and asked, "Would you take our picture, Mr. Rhodes?"

Claude honed his gaze on Lexa for a few seconds, after which he turned toward CK and solemnly answered, "Sure."

"Great!" CK handed Claude his phone. "Just press this button when you're ready to take the picture."

"Got it," Claude said, and CK hurried back to the others.

"C'mon, squeeze together now," Claude said, fiddling with CK's phone.

Palmer leaned against Paige and wrapped his arms tightly around her waist.

Paige forced an inch or two distance between her rear and Palmer's front. She exchanged her smirk for a sultry pout. "My, my, Palmer, I just felt how excited you are. And to think I felt you didn't even want to come."

Palmer pressed up against Paige's rear again. "I

didn't, but I always rise to the occasion for my friends."

Paige broke away from Palmer's grasp and turned to face him. "You need to keep it in your pants, lover boy. You don't have enough assets to acquire these goods."

"Maybe, but I know who does," Palmer said, matter-of-factly winning the verbal joust.

CK stood behind Cassie and helped her face the camera. "Just look that way," he instructed. After a second or two, he caught his faux pas and blurted out, "Sorry, Cass, I meant…"

Cassie patted CK's hand. "I know what you meant," she said. "I'm just glad to be facing the camera for once."

Bastian moved over and stood next to Lexa, who finally turned away from her brother. "I don't like boats," he whispered. His pent-up anxiety made his voice crack. "Ever since I was a kid, I've never liked boats."

"That's okay," Lexa said. "We all have skeletons left over from childhood." She turned toward Alex and motioned for her brother to come stand next to her but he shook his head and remained where he was. Voices in the young woman's head accused her of abandoning her twin on a holiday. They'd never spent one apart.

"Okay…" said Claude, holding up the camera phone.

Lexa tried to ignore the voices and plastered on a "happy face."

CK snuck a quick peek at Lexa, one that seemed to last for an eternity, for within that moment, years of unrequited love for this young woman erupted from his heart and splashed before his eyes.

"Smile!" Claude took several pictures and then handed the phone back to CK.

Lexa ran over and hugged her uncle again before rejoining the others.

"You guys watch out for each other!" Claude called after them.

"Don't worry, we'll be fine," CK assured him.

Claude waved and headed for his car. Alex inched his way close to Lexa and stood at her side. The sadness behind his eyes was too much for him to suppress.

Tears streamed down Lexa's face as her eyes took in her twin brother's pain. She paused for a brief time to compose herself. Afterwards she turned toward her waiting friends and said, "You guys go on inside. I'll catch up to you in a minute."

"Okay, we'll wait for you," CK said, and he and the others headed into the landing.

Lexa took hold of Alex's hands. "Always?" She placed his right hand over her heart, the first part of a ritual they'd been doing since they were kids.

"Always," Alex repeated. "Forever?" Alex brought up Lexa's right hand and placed it over his heart.

"Forever," finished Lexa. When she started to move her hand, Alex took it and pressed it firmly back over his heart.

"Forever isn't long enough," Alex said with grave intensity. They shared a moment of closeness that only twins could understand. A closeness that could only be reached by sharing the same womb.

Alex's hand wrapped around the locket resting against Lexa's heart. He held it up and gave it a kiss before putting it back down against his sister's chest.

Lexa embraced Alex and gazed into his eyes, which were red and brimming with tears. As she prepared to say goodbye, her brother shushed her.

"Never say goodbye," he said. "Say 'later' instead. Goodbyes are for people you'll never see again."

"Okay. Later, X-Man."

"Later, Sis."

After a painful moment, Lexa turned and headed toward the landing.

Love. Why can something that brings so much joy also cause so much pain?

The further away she got from her twin, the stronger the pain grew inside of her head. Lexa stopped halfway, took a large prescription medicine bottle out of her purse, opened the bottle, and took a dose. After taking a calming exhale, she shoved the bottle back into her purse and hurried up the stairs. All the while, Alex stood watching until Lexa disappeared into the landing.

CHAPTER FOUR

PASSAGE

Lexa hurried through the landing and caught up with the others waiting by the boarding gate.

CK took a step toward her and raised his brow. "You ready for this?" he asked with the zeal of a second grader about to go on a field trip.

"Um, yeah," Lexa said. *Yeah, sure I am.* "Can't wait to get there."

"I thought you might have had a change of mind," Paige taunted.

Lexa shot her friend a puzzled look. "Huh? About what?"

"About coming this weekend."

"Oh no. I wouldn't miss this for the world."

Paige gave her friend a nudge and motioned to the boarding agent standing patiently in front of them.

The boarding agent took their VIP tickets before leading the group toward the Catalina Express, an elegant vessel flaunting polished white fiberglass and dark privacy windows.

"Is it big?" Cassie asked with meek enthusiasm.

"Yeah, it's about a hundred footer," CK answered.

"One hundred and two feet to be exact," the boarding agent chimed in. "It happens to be the newest addition to our fleet. As a matter of fact—"

Palmer stuffed a twenty-dollar bill into the agent's pocket, cutting him off. "Thanks for the stats, chief. That was most interesting."

When they reached the gangplank, a steward greeted the party. "Welcome aboard! I am Roger, one of your personal stewards for the day. Senator Storm himself has asked the captain to make your trip with us one to remember." He politely ushered them aboard.

The passenger decks were teeming with tourists, making them standing room only. Screaming children and chattering parents drowned out the sound of the waves crashing against the ship's hull. A portly couple battling a bout of seasickness scrambled past on their way to the restrooms.

"Pretty nice," Bastian remarked.

"Nice?" Palmer snickered. "It's a floating metro line."

Paige shot daggers at her pretentious friend.

Palmer glanced around at the gaggle of boisterous passengers and said, "You'd think the good senator would have the graft to charter us a private yacht."

"Give Spence a chance," Paige said, rushing to the senator's defense. "I mean, he just got elected."

"Spence?" Bastian said, his tone dripping with

spite. He moved closer to his friend and muttered, "Don't worry, Palmer, *Spence* is getting plenty of graft these days—and nights."

The steward nervously cleared his throat after that last remark and opened the door to the captain's lounge, a spacious entertaining area with large bay windows, leather couches and chairs, and fine cherry hardwood tables. The lounge was adorned with brightly colored balloons and a huge banner that read: **'KUDOS MAG SEVEN.'** Upon the bar sat several silver champagne buckets, and the tables were loaded with party trays filled with caviar and cheeses, meats, breads, and condiments for sandwiches.

"Now this is more like it," said Palmer. He tipped the steward a couple of twenties. "I gotta hand it to him. Storm is a man of his word." Palmer opened his custom leather pack and took out a very old and very expensive bottle of Dom Perignon champagne...

***

On election night, Spencer Storm's campaign headquarters buzzed with uncontrollable excitement. Throngs of campaign workers and their families and friends scampered about the large office space. Workstations and tables stacked with office equipment were half hidden by the streamers and confetti covering them. Three one hundred inch high definition televisions equidistantly positioned around the room displayed the evening's latest returns, which showed Storm winning by a seventy percent margin.

Amidst all of this chaos, the newly elected senator's family sat quietly on one of the sofas in the middle of the room.

"Mommy, does that mean Daddy won?" asked Mariah Storm, Spencer's four-year-old daughter.

"Yes it does, my darling," replied the six-month pregnant Melissa Storm. She looked down at her daughter, and then at her one-year-old son Dylan asleep in her arms. "Yes, it does!" Around Mrs. Storm's sofa stood Lexa, Kimberly, Palmer, Bastian, Cassie, and CK—six out of the seven members of her husband's inner circle.

Lexa gave Melissa a big hug. "I'm so happy for you and your family, Mel. You all have a great future ahead of you."

"Thank you, sweetie." She scanned the room for her husband, but didn't see him. "Lexa, would you please hold Dylan for a moment? I want to go find my husband and tell him the good news."

"Um, sure."

As Melissa prepared to hand her baby to Lexa, Bastian jumped up and said, "Don't trouble yourself, Mrs. S. I'll go get him. I think I know right where he is."

"That's all right, Bastian. I'll—"

"It's no bother. Besides, Lexa doesn't have a maternal bone in her body." Bastian patted Lexa on her shoulder then took off into the cheering crowd.

Melissa and Lexa looked at each other and grinned. "He's never going to change, is he?" asked Melissa.

"I sincerely doubt it," Lexa said.

A few minutes later, Bastian returned with Senator Storm, who was parting a sea of admiring supporters. Storm rushed over to his wife and gave her a big kiss on her lips, and then on her expectant stomach. After pecking Dylan on the cheek, he picked up Mariah, gave her a kiss, and put her on his hip. "Hold on a minute, everyone. Hold on!" Storm shouted above the accolades roaring from the crowd. After the uproar settled, Storm set his daughter down beside his wife and pointed up at one of the three large screen televisions announcing his victory. "That right there isn't just my victory. That victory belongs to each and every person in this room!" The crowd roared again, then quieted when Storm pointed back up at the screen. "That right there is the result of months of long, hard work from everyone in this room…"

While Storm carried on with his speech, Lexa noticed that Paige was absent from their troupe of seven gathered in front of the Storms. She glanced around the crowded room before asking just above a whisper, "Where's Paige?"

"What? She's not here? Narcissistic bitch," Palmer muttered.

CK scanned the room. "Anybody see her?"

"Nope, not me," Cassie replied.

"Maybe one of us should go look for her," Kimberly suggested. "No telling how long Storm is going to rattle on before turning the spotlight on us."

"I've got it," Bastian said with clear irritation. He made a beeline for the supply room.

Kimberly whispered to Lexa, "Is he her minder

now?"

"I know, right?" Lexa remarked. While she and Kimberly giggled to themselves, Bastian returned with Paige in tow.

Kimberly grabbed Paige by the arm and whispered, "Where have you been?"

Paige subtly cut her eyes at Melissa Storm, whose stealthy glare immediately caught the young woman's glance.

"But there were seven of you who went above and beyond the call of duty," Storm said. "Seven of you who stood out as leaders who practically moved into this office and called it home over the course of the campaign. These seven's tireless and unrelenting devotion to this campaign earned them a special nickname, that they proved they deserved time and time again." Storm motioned to Lexa and the others. "Here they are folks! Lexa Rhodes, Kimberly Clark, Cassie Lovette, Paige Turner, Palmer Randolph, Bastian Shadwell, and Christopher Kane—the Magnificent Seven!" As the room erupted with applause, Storm gathered his inner circle around him. "I promise that each and every one of you will be well rewarded. And also, I invite you all to continue on as members of my staff."

The members of the Magnificent Seven hooted and congratulated each other.

***

"Tonight's toast deserves only the best," Palmer said while the others oohed and aahed and then applauded. He carefully uncorked the bottle of Dom Perignon and began filling the seven crystal champagne flutes.

Paige handed Lexa a glass. "Looks like you could use this."

Lexa took the glass and set it down on the table in front of her. "I better not, it might interact with my meds."

"C'mon, one drink won't kill you," Bastian chided. "Besides, you owe it to the new senator, and to us." He picked up the glass and put it back into Lexa's hand.

"Okay, just one." Lexa gulped. *Yeah, one drink won't kill me.*

"That's my girl," said Bastian.

Palmer poured himself some champagne and stood. "Okay, okay, okay, everybody. Here's to Senator Storm for inviting us to Catalina on this Thanksgiving holiday, to celebrate his recent election victory." He held up his glass in toast. "Cheers!" Everyone except Lexa took a sip of Palmer's "I'm someone with money" champagne. Then he picked up the glass set aside for Kimberly and said, "And to us, the Magnificent Seven, minus one. The driving force behind the good senator's victory. Cheers!"

"Cheers!" the rest chimed in before downing their drinks with one swift gulp. They lowered their empty glasses and saw Lexa was still holding a full glass.

Lexa held up her glass. "Cheers." The apprehension in her voice matched the uncertainty in her head.

What would Alex do? He'd tell me to go on, it's just one little toast.

Following a fleeting stint of indecision, Lexa took a healthy swig of champagne. The others applauded.

See? No prob.

It only took a few moments for the alcohol to start affecting her body's chemistry.

Bastian poured himself another glass of champagne, then set the glass down after almost belching up his previous mouthful. Palmer gleefully patted his friend's back while taking a big bite out of his dry salami sandwich.

"What's the matter, Ahab?" he asked Bastian. "Bit of trouble with the ol' sea legs?"

"Fuck you, asshole," he retorted raggedly. "I told you...I don't like boats."

"How many have you been on?"

"I've never been on one."

Palmer snickered. "No wonder you're in a bad way. Nothing'll screw you up faster than popping a cherry." When Palmer laughed, his gaze fell upon Lexa. He straightened up and said patronizingly, "I'm sorry, I meant having one's first experience." Lexa shook her head and smirked with feigned amusement. "Ha, ha, ha."

"First times suck, don't let anyone tell you any different," Bastian advised.

"I know, right?" Lexa said in heartfelt agreement. *Some more than others.* Already starting to feel a bit woozy herself, she sat down next to one of the lounge's bay windows. A deafening silence crept upon her as her eyes were dazzled by the chaotic rhythm of the churning waves. Back and forth. Side to side. Back and forth. Side to side. More than half of the ship's passengers were succumbing to seasickness as large ground swells rocked the vessel like a toy boat navigating the turbulence of a hyperactive child's bathtub. However, instead of dredging up the remains of her last meal, the incessant ocean motion was stirring long-forgotten mental images buried deep in the recesses of Lexa's mind. While those around her regurgitated a bile-laced stew of partial digestion, her psyche vomited up suppressed memories from a misplaced childhood…

***

Darkness. Emptiness. Nothingness. No thought, no self-awareness or identity. And then there was a voice. A soothing yet commanding voice that echoed from beyond the void.

"Five…four…"

A consciousness began spiraling out of oblivion.

Is this real? Someone please tell me. Am I real?

The disembodied voice neared the end of its countdown. "Three…two…"

The consciousness cleared the dark center of the vortex.

Where am I? Who am I?

"One."

I am…

"Lexa, open your eyes," the voice commanded.

I am Lexa…

Eight-year-old Lexa opened her eyes. She saw a

large computer monitor placed directly in front of her, and upon its screen swirled a black and white animated hypnotic spiral.

"How are you feeling right now?"

"I'm okay," Lexa answered. "Just a little dizzy." Her pupils widely dilated from the monitor's penetrating glow, she surveyed the darkened room but was unable to discover the source of the voice addressing her. Lexa's feeling of curiosity was being replaced by a creeping sense of apprehension. "Who are you?"

"Don't you remember? I'm Dr. Cross." A desk lamp switched on to reveal James Cross, a lean blond man in his mid-fifties with chiseled features.

Lexa tried to grasp what was happening. "How...?"

"How what?"

"How did I get here?"

"Your Aunt Amanda brought you here."

"Aunt Amanda?"

"Yes. I've been working with your brother for a while now, but this is your first time with me."

"Why am I here?"

"Because now I'll be working with you as well."

"What are you and Alex working on?" Lexa asked with childish innocence.

"Oh, just some things your parents thought Alex needed help with." Cross's eyes locked on his young patient's face, attempting to detect any signs of emotional response, but there were none. "Does he ever talk to you about me, or our time together?"

Lexa shook her head. "Nope." *I wish he was here with me now.* "Where is Alex?"

35

"He's in the waiting room with your aunt."

"Can he come in here with me?"

"It's better if he doesn't," Cross replied. "This is our time, Lexa." He switched off his desk lamp, which once again made the computer's monitor the only source of illumination. "I'll be spending time with your brother later."

An eerie feeling of recognition washed across Lexa's cerebral cortex.

I do remember Alex telling me about him. Alex said that I should never talk to him, that I should never trust him.

"I don't wanna be here. I wanna go home."

"Now, now, Lexa. Your aunt wouldn't have brought you here if she didn't think—"

"I wanna go home!"

After a brief moment of hesitation, from behind the spiraling screen Cross's voice picked up where it left off. "Home, Lexa?"

"Yes, please. Please let me go home."

"What is home, Lexa?"

Home? Why it's...it's...home?

A startling inability to remember overwhelmed the young girl's sense of understanding. "Um…"

"The place you call home, what is it? Where is it?"

Tears streamed down Lexa's face. "I…I don't know." The terror of this realization sent her heart rate racing and shallowed her breathing. She jumped up out of her chair and scanned the dimmed room for an exit. "I want my Mommy and Daddy!" she cried.

"Mommy and Daddy aren't here," Cross said.

"I want my Mommy and Daddy. I want my Mommy and Daddy. I want my Mommy and Daddy!"

"Your Mommy and Daddy are dead, Lexa," Cross said calmly.

The harsh bluntness of the information's release loosened Lexa's hold on sanity. "No!" she wailed, pacing frantically in the semi-darkness. "They're not dead. They're not! They're not... They're not dead..."

***

Memories flashed before Lexa's teary eyes, memories that seemed as resolutely distant as the black-hole center of the spiraling vortex facing her.

Daddy laughed...Mommy smiled...Alex played...Lexa ran...Dinner cooked. Presents opened. Alex played. Lexa ran. Voices raised. Children listened. Alex played. Lexa ran. Flames erupted. Doors burned. Walls fell. Voices screamed. Bodies burned. Lexa screamed. Sirens blared. Lights flashed...

***

Stop it, Lexa. Don't remember.

"No. They're not dead. They're not..." Lexa's eyes darted around the room in a desperate attempt to find her twin brother. " Alex! Help me, Alex! Help me."

"There's nothing Alex can do to help you. What

do you think he's going to do, bring your parents back from the dead?"

"They're not dead!" Lexa shrieked. "They're not!"

"They are, Lexa. You must remember," Cross said in a tone rich with uncompromising insistence.

"I don't remember!" *I won't remember!* "I don't remember!"

"Lexa—"

"And you can't make me!"

"Lexa, listen to me," Cross pleaded.

"Alex, help me!" Lexa screamed. "Help me, Alex, please! Help me…"

Darkness. Emptiness. Nothingness. No thought, no self-awareness or identity. And then there was Cross's voice counting from beyond the void. "Five…four…"

Lexa's consciousness began spiraling out of oblivion. *No! Please let me stay here…*

"Three…two…"

Lexa's consciousness cleared the dark center of the vortex. *No…I don't want to—*

"One."

No. Not again…

"Lexa, open your eyes."

***

Lexa opened her eyes and stared out through the large bay windows at the foam-crested waves churning just beneath her. She opened her purse and took out one of her bottles of prescription medicine. With shaking hands, she held up the bottle and read the label: *DO NOT TAKE WITH ALCOHOL.* She shoved the bottle back into her purse and grabbed hold of the locket hanging around her neck.

I wish you were here with me now.

Lexa opened the locket to reveal a picture of Alex at age eight facing a picture of herself at the same age.

I *guess I'm the forever of your always, or vice versa.* Lexa chuckled to herself. *But you know what? I wouldn't have it any other way.*

"What's up!" Bastian screamed into her ear, almost knocking the unprepared young woman onto the cabin's floor.

"Goddammit, Bastian!" Lexa screamed. "What's *wrong* with you?"

Bastian smirked. "Plenty, but that's beside the point."

"Did you have to scare me out of my wits?"

Bastian grinned and bobbed with childish fervor.

"Sorry, babe," Paige said. "But since you wouldn't join the party, the party decided to join you."

Bastian, Paige, and the others yanked Lexa up from her chair and found a place for her in their skewed lineup, then they all performed an impromptu conga line while Gloria Estefan's song "Conga" blasted through the cabin's recessed speakers.

CHAPTER FIVE

SANTA CATALINA

The Catalina Express docked at Avalon Harbor. The six present members of the Magnificent Seven disembarked with subdued enthusiasm, their excitement cooled and energy expended by too much alcohol and conga dancing. Standing on the dock was a limo driver holding a sign reading: **'MAG 7.'**

"Nice touch, Storm, nice touch," Palmer remarked in an "I'm not that impressed" tone after he noticed the appreciative expressions on the others' faces.

The six friends piled into the limousine, the driver closed the doors, and proceeded to assist the Express's porters in packing the first load of their luggage into the trunk.

After a scenic drive, the limousine pulled into the driveway of a secluded five bedroom beach-front villa, the best available in Harrington Cove, an exclusive Spanish-themed gated community that offered some of the most luxurious and costly vacation rentals the island had to offer. The driver hopped out, hurrying over to open the passenger door.

Paige exited the limo and winked at him. "Thanks, sweetie. I *really* enjoyed the ride." Her sultry banter and flirtatious airs were offered in lieu of a monetary tip, which the driver gladly accepted.

Lexa got out next and stumbled backward into the driver. "Sorry," she said as he steadied her and helped her back on her feet. "Whoa. I guess I shouldn't have had that drink after all." After she composed herself, Lexa turned and got an eyeful of the extravagant ocean view villa, a three-story luxury house crowned with weathered, red-orange Spanish tiles. A fresh coat of white paint made the villa stand out from the surrounding flora as if it was being lit by a spotlight at night. "Is this where we're staying?"

"Nice, isn't it? Spence has good taste," said Paige, who was referring more to herself than the villa. She grinned and slapped herself on her rear end.

When the driver opened the trunk, Bastian and CK hurried over to the front of the limo to get a full view of the villa.

"Holy shit!" Bastian exclaimed excitedly, putting his hand on CK's shoulder. "Call my mom and tell her to send my things 'cause I'm never going home."

"Right after I call mine," CK crowed.

Cassie unfolded her white cane and stood beside the limo. "So what's the place like?"

41

CK whistled. "It's sweeeeeeet."

"Sweet?" Bastian echoed. "It's lifestyles of the rich and fucking famous!"

"It's adequate," Palmer said, maintaining his signature air of indifference.

After the driver finished unloading the luggage and closed the trunk, Palmer held out a fifty-dollar bill.

"No need for a tip, sir," the driver said. "It's already been taken care of."

Palmer shrugged and put the money into his pocket.

Bastian snatched the fifty out of Palmer's pocket and shoved it into the driver's hand. "Go ahead," he said, "I insist."

"Thank you, sir. I'll go retrieve the rest of your luggage and have it here within the hour."

"Thank you, my good man," Bastian mocked with an excessively pretentious accent.

Palmer, speechless from being so easily shown up, shot Bastian a heated glare as the driver got into the limousine and drove away.

***

The six members of Senator Storm's Magnificent Seven entered the villa. The vaulted ceilings, marble floors, and adorned walls framed an eye-pleasing layout of posh and expensive furniture. A bounty of wrapped gifts spread in front of the roaring, wood-burning fireplace was the icing on the senator's "gratitude cake" for their work on the campaign, a hearty thanks for a job well done.

Lexa walked over and sat alone in a corner trying to ward off a building headache.

"The chauffeur said there's four bedrooms, each with its own bathroom, and a master suite," Cassie announced, sweeping her white cane from side to side. "So the question before us now is who's going to sleep with who?"

Lexa snuck a glance at CK. *Hmmm, might not be such a bad weekend after all.* When CK caught her stare, Lexa bashfully averted her eyes. *Yeah right, like a guy that cute could like a girl as socially inept as I.*

"I'll take the master suite," Palmer said with affluent attitude.

"Like hell you will," Paige snapped from the fully-stocked mahogany wet bar. "The master is mine. You might be nouveau riche, but my blood is blue, kiddo."

"Guys, guys, instead of fighting over it, why don't you two share the room for the weekend?" Cassie lightheartedly suggested. "I'm sure there's enough room."

Palmer put his hand to his chin and tapped on his lips with his index finger, his eyes giving Paige a long and lecherous once-over. "Well...if it'll keep the peace, I guess I can make the sacrifice. Besides, it probably has a California King bed."

Paige shook her head and let out a laugh dripping with unadulterated conceit. "Yeah right." She sauntered over to Lexa and wrapped her arms around her coy friend. "Mmmm..." Paige turned back toward Palmer and licked her lips seductively. "Besides, if I decided to share my bed with a friend,

43

it wouldn't be you." She turned back to Lexa. "I've always wanted to do this," she quietly confessed before leaning in and giving her bemused friend a soft, sensual kiss.

"Fuck me," Bastian breathed from his gaping mouth.

"You and me both," added Palmer breathlessly.

While CK stood staring longingly at Paige helping herself to Lexa's full, moist lips, Cassie tugged on his arm and asked in a low voice, "What's going on?"

Yes, what the hell is going on?

After hearing her blind friend's softly spoken question, Lexa pulled away from Paige and cast her eyes downward in stunned embarrassment.

Paige gave Palmer a self-assured wink. "Guess that's settled then, yes?"

Palmer feigned applause and bowed to Paige in capitulation. The ensuing moment of uncomfortable silence was brought to an end by Bastian saying, "Looks like Christmas has come early." He motioned to the beautifully wrapped presents stacked in front of the fireplace. "What do ya say we leave the room assignments for later and go check out what ol' Saint Spence has left for us?" Bastian beckoned for the others to follow him.

Paige, CK, Cassie, and Palmer made their way toward the fireplace, but Lexa stayed put in her lonesome corner.

Noticing his friend's reticence, Bastian called out, "Lexa?"

Lexa turned around and caught Bastian's questioning stare. "Yes?"

"Gonna join the party?"

"I'll be there after a while, okay?"

"Suit yourself."

Suit myself? I wish I could.

In hopes of alleviating the physical pain from her mounting headache, and the emotional pain from her separation from Alex, Lexa decided to go off and have some alone time away from the others, who were gathered around the fireplace tearing into more spoils from the Senator.

***

Lexa strolled out onto a sunlit balcony with a view only those willing to pay through the nose would ever see. The salty ocean wind blowing through her made her think of all the times she wished to be free, to have her own life, away from Aunt Amanda, Uncle Claude, Dr. Cross and yes, even Alex.

Without Alex?

She took her locket out of her purse and opened it...

***

Carl and Lisa Rhodes screamed at each other from inside the family's cabin. It was the kind of screaming that generated terror in the fear center of a child's brain, the same type of innate terror as the thought of a closet monster or the thing underneath the bed. It was this kind of terror that stopped eight-year-old Lexa and Alex from playing their game of hide-and-seek and focused their attention on the commotion coming from inside the cabin. A deep feeling of sorrow intermixed with the young twins' terror as they began to understand the nature of their parents' argument.

***

A cool wind cascaded over the isolated balcony, and Lexa rubbed her thumb across her locket.

I'm so tired of looking back. Why can't I just look forward?

She noticed some kids stoking a fire pit on the beach below.

***

"Mommy! Daddy!" screamed little Lexa as the cabin was engulfed in orange flames.

Alex, Mommy, and Daddy were burning inside. They were still inside! The raging fire heated the salty tears streaking her face as she stood and helplessly watched…

***

The intensity of that memory compelled Lexa to tightly shut her eyes. When she opened them, CK was standing right beside her.

"Jesus!" she exclaimed as she was jolted back to reality.

"Sorry," CK said. "Didn't mean to go stalker on you." He was holding a drink in each hand. "You okay? You seem a little—"

"I'm fine," Lexa said, although her tone indicated she really wasn't. She gazed off toward the horizon and whispered, "Just missing my brother."

CK offered Lexa a drink, but she pushed it away. He took a sip of his drink, sneaking a peek at the locket Lexa was holding.

Lexa noticed CK eyeing her locket and shut it.

***

The head chef lowered a turkey into a forty-quart stock pot in the food preparation area of the beach banquet setup which was halfway between their villa and the Cove's common area. He covered the pot full of boiling peanut oil and adjusted the temperature gauge on the propane tank. He and his assistants were wearing protective aprons, safety goggles, gloves, and oversized chef's hats. A second covered pot sat ten feet away frying another turkey. Two fire extinguishers and a first aid kit lay between the two pots, in case of any unlikely mishaps.

The event manager approached the food prep area and walked over to the head chef with all the manner and presence of a boot camp drill sergeant. "Is everything going according to schedule?"

"Yes sir," the head chef answered in a wannabe Maurice Chevalier French accent. He slapped on a subservient guise, and then scowled after his boss walked away.

***

About half a mile down the beach from the Mag Seven's private villa, which was the property's premiere rental, was Harrington Cove's extravagant common area, complete with an Olympic size pool and a beachside bar. It was full of residents and vacationers who represented the Cove's bourgeoisie, mere commoners in comparison to the haughty few privileged enough to reside where the Mag Seven were staying.

Bastian and Paige showed up at the bar dressed to the nines.

"Wow! Look who's all dressed up for once," Paige joked.

"Ah gee, Paige," Bastian exclaimed with brazen derision. "That sure means a lot coming from you, considering how much I respect your opinion."

A few moments later, CK and Cassie arrived.

"Wow, CK, you look good enough to eat," Paige said with a flirtatious wink.

"Literally or figuratively?" CK frigidly responded. She wasn't his type.

Cassie giggled as CK led her to a barstool and helped her sit down.

"At least four of Storm's Magnificent Seven are here," Cassie said. "Think that'll satisfy the good senator?"

"I doubt it," Paige said. "Spence is an all or nothing kind of guy."

"Oh really? And how would you know that?"

asked Cassie with a hint of sarcasm. "Are the rumors 'round the water cooler true after all?"

"I'm sure I have no idea what you're talking about," Paige replied with a less-than-convincing inflection.

"Spoken in true political fashion," CK said, pulling out a stool and sitting down. "When cornered, always plead the fifth."

Paige scanned the area. "What's keeping the others?"

"Lexa's still getting dressed," Cassie told her. "I don't know where Palmer is."

CK shook his head and snickered. "I saw him a few minutes ago by the pool talking to one of those wannabe French waitresses."

Just then he noticed a hooded chef carrying a large bag. The faceless chef caught CK's stare, then turned and faced the young man staring at him from the bar. God only knew what was staring from underneath that hood, which completely concealed the chef's head, giving him the appearance of someone you wouldn't want to run into in a dark alley. The hairs on the back of CK's neck began to stand on end. After what seemed like a long, long while, the chef headed for the cooking area and stood next to one of the stock pots.

"Still with us, CK?" Paige prompted.

CK snapped out of his stupor. "Did you guys see…" He paused, not knowing how to finish his question without sounding like he was paranoid.

"Um, I know you're not asking me," Cassie joked.

"See what?" asked Bastian.

"Nothing," CK said.

Half out of breath and full of anxious energy, Lexa ran up and joined the others. "Am I late?"

"Not quite, but nice try," Paige quipped.

Bastian cleared his throat. "Not meaning to piss on our parade, but there's two of our seven who are still MIA, and the clock is ticking."

Lexa glanced at her watch. Where were the others? They should have arrived by now. And where was Kimmy? "I'm going to look for Palmer," she said, hurrying away.

Paige laughed. "Guess we're back down to a foursome." Paige sexed up her voice. "Two guys, two girls—Mmmm—one of my favorite combinations."

***

At the pool area, Palmer sat talking with one of the waitresses. He casually brought his left hand up to his face, causing light to reflect off his Rolex with deal-sealing intensity. If she didn't know he had money, she sure as hell knew now. The light drew the waitress's attention to Palmer's expensive timepiece.

"The old adage is still true, you know. It's not what you know, but who you know," Palmer said with such flagrant pretension one would think he must have been formally schooled in it.

While he worked to secure his latest conquest, Lexa made her way to the pool area. Neurons inside her head were firing with the same speed and intensity as the sky bursts of a Fourth of July fireworks finale.

How can I cut the cord? It's so...so thick?

Behind Lexa's pretty face waged a fierce battle, one that would have no winners. Would accepting the senator's job offer cost her her brother?

After strolling aimlessly amongst a sea of scantily clad strangers, Lexa spotted Palmer. When she started toward him, her smartphone chimed, alerting her to a text message. She took the phone out of her purse and checked the screen.

KIMBERLY: Sorry I'm running late. See you at dinner.

The same chef CK saw stood facing Lexa from across the pool. After casually taking in her surroundings, the woman was taken aback when she spotted the hooded chef facelessly staring at her. She started to look away, but for some unknown reason was drawn—no, *compelled*—to stare back at the foreboding figure standing across from her. The hooded chef was clutching an empty bag. He meticulously folded the bag, pocketed it, and disappeared into the crowd.

After regaining her composure, Lexa headed to where Palmer sat chatting with a waitress. She walked up behind him and tapped his head. "Let's go," she said, taking his arm. "We're running late."

"Okay, I'm coming." Palmer glanced down at his Rolex. He took the waitress's hand and projected his best alpha male aura. "Why don't we meet later for cocktails? What time do you—" Before Palmer could finish his proposition, Lexa yanked him up by his arm and briskly led him away. "That was uncalled for," he said petulantly.

"But necessary. Now move it," Lexa responded. "You better not make us late."

***

Lexa and Palmer joined Paige, Cassie, CK, and Bastian at the bar.

Bastian got up off his stool and offered it to Lexa. "Well maybe 'Triple S' won't notice we've decreased to the Magnificent Six, you think?" Bastian flippantly asked.

"Save it, Sebastian," Lexa said. "Kimber sent a text saying she'll be here any minute."

The event manager rushed up and motioned for Lexa and her friends to follow him back to their villa.

***

Cylindrical stand-up electric heaters warmed the cool November air of the private banquet on the beach. A full moon crested the horizon as Lexa, Paige, Palmer, and Bastian took their assigned seats at the lavish Thanksgiving table. CK helped Cassie find her chair, then sat down in his.

In the food preparation area, the head chef and two of his assistants approached one of the stock pots. He uncovered the pot and carefully lifted the turkey out of the boiling oil.

Terrence Simms, the senator's frail and formally

attired, red-headed right-hand man, entered the dining area. He straightened his tie and then hurried over to Lexa and the others. "Four, five, six," he counted. "Well it's good to see that almost all of you made it here tonight."

"I'm sorry, Mr. Simms, Kimber's running a little late," Lexa apologized.

Simms bent down close to Lexa and whispered, "Well she better show or it's her ass." Simms straightened up, adjusted his tie, then hurried to the head of the table.

Senator Spencer Storm, a handsome, charismatic man with enough JFK appeal to seize the lion's share of the state's women's votes, arrived on scene. As the senator and his cliché duo of security agents made their way through the crowded banquet area, Simms snatched up a wireless microphone and rushed toward him. When he reached Storm he looked up at him gleefully, like a child in awe. The senator gave his assistant a simple nod. Simms eagerly returned the senator's greeting and motioned to the event manager, who turned off the music and turned up the lights.

"Lexa," Paige whispered, trying in vain to get her friend's attention. "Lexa!" she whispered louder, loud enough to receive a scathing look from Simms.

The six members of the Mag Seven and the rest of those in attendance hushed and settled in their seats and Simms began his impromptu speech. "Ladies and gentlemen, we are gathered here tonight to celebrate a victory. One which all of you helped to bring about." Applause rang out, then died down. "When Spencer Storm won the senatorial election two weeks ago, it wasn't just his own personal victory, it was a victory for everyone in this state." More applause. "So now, without further ado, I present your host, Senator Spencer Storm!"

"Lexa," Paige said loudly enough to be heard by all those around her.

Lexa shushed her and turned back toward their arriving host.

Senator Storm and his entourage entered the dining area amidst applause from his guests and serving staff. Walking to the head of the table, he shook Simms's hand, then winked at Lexa and the rest of the group. "Thank you, thank you for your applause. Now let me applaud you, my friends, for if it weren't for the talented efforts of all of you here tonight I'd have no victory to celebrate."

While everyone applauded, Paige regained Lexa's attention and asked, "Where's Kimber?"

Lexa shrugged.

In the food prep area, the head chef and his assistants carried the sizzling turkey over to the serving table and placed it on a platter.

Storm turned toward the Mag Seven and winked. "And now to give credit where it's due"

The head chef and his assistants headed toward the other steaming stock pot.

"Our victory two weeks ago was brought about by a grassroots campaign that reached out to the hearts and minds of everyone in this state," Storm went on. "Its message of positive change transcended gender, ethnic, and religious barriers…"

The head chef reached the pot and carefully removed its lid.

"That campaign was the brainchild of seven gifted young campaign workers. These young people truly lived up to the nickname I gave them some months ago..."

The assistants aided the head chef as he prepared to lift the turkey out of the boiling pot.

"Ladies and gentlemen, I give you the Magnificent Seven!" Lexa, Paige, CK, Cassie, Bastian, and Palmer stood and accepted a round of applause.

The head chef shrieked in horror, after which the pot tipped over and splattered him with boiling peanut oil.

The pain-ridden screaming interrupted the Mag Seven's accolade and drew the attention of all to the food prep area.

The assistant chefs looked on in horror as their boss danced wildly around in spastic gyrations before dropping and writhing on the ground.

The two security agents whisked Storm away from the Thanksgiving banquet while the event manager pulled out his cell phone and dialed 911.

The six present members of the Mag Seven rushed to the preparation area and found the head chef curled up and twitching on the ground. When Lexa turned away from the awful sight, she saw the assistants motioning toward a spot on the beach. She looked down, then screamed and dropped to her knees. As Paige and CK rushed over to Lexa, Bastian's eyes fell upon a sight that sent him into a momentary state of shock.

"Look!" he shouted, grabbing Palmer's arm and pointing to Kimber's severed, fried head sizzling on the sand.

CHAPTER SIX

A QUESTION OF STYLES

The Avalon sheriff's station's main interrogation room had all the features one would expect to find: bare white walls, a large two-way mirror, and a metal table with two metal folding chairs.

Lexa sat restlessly at the table while two FBI agents observed her from different positions in the room.

"Tell us again about the hooded chef," said Agent #1.

Lexa glanced at her reflection in the large two-way mirror. "I saw one of the chefs staring at me. He was wearing a large hood that covered his head and most of his face."

"If the hood covered his face, how could you tell he was staring at you?" asked Agent #2.

Think, Lexa. How could you tell?

"I don't know." She tried to suppress the nausea building in her stomach that now heralds the arrival of one of her mind-splitting headaches. "I just...I could feel him looking at me."

Agent #1 asked, "Did the hooded chef have anything with him?"

"I don't know. I can't remember."

"CK told us he saw a hooded chef carrying some kind of bag," Agent #2 said.

"Oh yeah, he had a bag. Or a knapsack or something," Lexa said, glancing back at the two-way mirror.

Agent #2 added, "Was it big enough to hold Ms. Clark's head?"

Shocked speechless by the bluntness of the question, Lexa lowered her head and wept into her hands.

"That's enough for now, Ms. Rhodes," said Agent #1 after he realized they'd gotten all they were going to get out of the young woman. "If we have any further questions, we'll contact you." He opened the doors and motioned for Lexa to leave.

Lexa stood and took one last look at her reflection in the two-way mirror before exiting the interrogation room.

***

Paige, CK, Cassie, Bastian, and Palmer ran up to meet Lexa when she stepped into the lobby.

"Are you okay?" Paige asked. "God, I can't believe what's going on."

Bastian struggled to mask his sorrow with derision. "Well believe it, sunshine. This isn't some fucking dream we're going to wake up from."

"Are they sure the head…" Cassie gulped, "that

it was Kimber?"

Lexa nodded. "The FBI said they identified her headless...her body inside her apartment."

"Shouldn't one of us call Kimber's parents and tell them?" Cassie said tremulously.

"I'm sure the cops have already told them," Palmer barked.

"Yeah, but we should still talk to them ourselves in person. We owe Kimber that much," CK said.

While Lexa and the others stood talking, Deputy Detective Scott Peters, a balding, overweight gentleman in his early fifties, approached them from behind.

"Before I let you go, there's one more person who wants to talk to you," he informed them.

Captain Marsha Styles, a tall brunette with an athletic build, entered the room. "Hello, I'm Marsha Styles, captain of the Long Beach Homicide Bureau. I know you've all been through a lot, so I'll make this brief." Captain Styles held up Lexa's cellphone. "You told the FBI you received a text message from Ms. Clark just minutes before her head was discovered."

"Yes."

"You also stated that Ms. Clark sent you a text this morning which said she had to deal with a personal matter, an ex-boyfriend I believe, and would catch a later shuttle."

CK took a step forward. "Yeah, I remember Lexa saying—"

Styles shushed CK, then turned back to Lexa.

"Uh, yes, Ms—Captain Styles."

Styles held up Lexa's phone. "You don't mind if

59

I keep this for a while, do you?"

Lexa shrugged. "Sure, go ahead."

Bastian smirked. "Like you have a choice," he mumbled.

Styles shot a scathing look at Bastian before saying to them all, "The whole island's under lockdown—no one in or out. We've checked out your villa and others surrounding it and they're all clear. Round-the-clock security has been arranged for you for the rest of your stay, courtesy of Senator Storm. That's all, for now. See you all at the funeral." Just after Captain Styles turned to leave, she stopped and turned back around. "There's just one thing I want to go over, to make sure I'm understanding it correctly." She strolled in front of the lineup of friends the way a drill sergeant does in front of new recruits. "Apart from the two text messages Ms. Rhodes received, none of you had any other contact with Ms. Clark, correct?" She stopped in front of Lexa, but didn't turn to face her.

"Correct," Lexa answered.

Styles closely examined her detainees' facial expressions, which ranged from pondering to umbrage, then faced forward and resumed her stroll. "No phone calls, nothing?"

"No," Cassie said timidly while the others simply shook their heads.

"Really? That's odd."

"Yeah? How so?" asked Palmer.

When Styles reached CK, the last person in line, she reversed her walk of inquiry.

"I'd have thought that at some point during the day at least one of you would have tried to reach her for a good ol' fashioned voice-to-voice phone call, if for no other reason than to see if she was on her way yet." Styles raised her eyebrows. "I mean, if it were me, at your age, and we were all on a swanky all-expense paid trip to a swanky island paradise with swanky private limo service and our own swanky private villa, and one of my good friends, who was also invited, missed the boat and was coming up later..." Styles paused and made eye contact with the two sighted girls of the bunch. She took a quick look at Cassie's white cane and carried on, "...I would imagine I'd be on the phone nonstop with my absent girlfriend, describing the captain's lounge, sending her inane selfies from inside the limo, telling her she won't believe how absolutely sick the villa is. You know, behavior typical of your generation." Even with her back to him, Palmer's muted scoff was caught by the captain's attentive ear. She whirled around to face him. "Did I say something you don't agree with, Mr. Randolph?"

"A couple of things," Palmer answered indignantly.

"Please, don't be afraid to speak your mind." Styles folded her arms and stood awaiting his response.

Sensing that his friend was gearing up to say something he would regret later, Bastian grabbed Palmer's shoulder and took a half step forward toward the captain. "Um, I think what my well-to-do friend here was about to disagree on was your overuse of the term 'swanky'." The untimely, but amusing, quip drew grins from all except Lexa and Cassie.

Styles approached Bastian like a Black Mamba slithering toward its next meal. "That's very funny. Think I'll start calling you Funny Man." Bastian cast his eyes downward and snickered. "Isn't it a shame though, Funny Man, that Ms. Clark isn't here to enjoy your levity along with the rest of us? Oh, that's right—she's dead, isn't she?" Bastian's grin dropped into a resentful frown.

"That was insensitive," Paige countered. "And completely uncalled for."

"No, Ms. Turner, what's insensitive and completely uncalled for is your friend lying in the county morgue with her head carved off with a hunting knife."

Cassie whimpered aloud. CK put his arm around her and then caught Styles's eye. "I wanna know what good you think this is doing?"

"Yeah?" Styles snapped. "Well, *I* wanna know why none of you bothered to call Ms. Clark on the phone today." She looks across the row of friends.

"Are you insinuating that one of us—"

"Of course not, Mr. Randolph. I'm just trying to wrap my head around this apparent lack of concern you all had for this supposed friend of yours."

"I don't know!" Cassie sobbed. "I don't know why any of us didn't call her!"

"What about the rest of you, huh?" The others lowered their eyes and stood in communal silence. "What about you, Ms. Rhodes? You and Ms. Clark were best friends, right?"

"Yes, we are. Were…" Lexa replied amidst a volley of quiet tears.

"Why didn't you try to call her?"

"I don't know." Lexa broke down into uncontrollable sobs.

"Not even one of you has a theory as to why?" Styles pressed.

"I guess we're all just a bunch of self-centered assholes," Bastian said with facetious spite.

"In your case, Mr. Shadwell, that's not theory, it's fact." Styles took a few steps back from the shell-shocked individuals and faced the group as a whole. "I promise you, this is just the beginning," she warned with dead seriousness. "A fucking monster killed your friend, and fucking monsters never go away. Not until somebody stops them." Captain Styles straightened her collar and trod off toward the interrogation room doors.

CHAPTER SEVEN

HOME SWEET HOME

Tired and overwrought from the day's dreadful events and Captain Styles' haughty manner and accusatory tone, the senator's six guests were taken by limo back to their villa. They entered the darkened foyer and for a long, lasting moment, stood in solemn silence. After a while they each came to realize they had inadvertently positioned themselves in a "missing man formation." The reality of Kimberly's murder crashed down upon them for the first time. The weight of this realization sent them trudging up to their rooms. Except for food runs to the kitchen, the six kept to their rooms for the next couple of days, each submerged in their own particular style of mourning. Lexa's sole coping strategy was taking extra doses of her anti-psychotics. After a forty-eight hour investigation produced no further leads, the island-wide detention was called off and the group was granted permission by Captain Styles to leave.

***

The six remaining members of the Magnificent Seven hardly spoke a word to each other on the boat ride back to Long Beach. When they arrived at the landing in downtown Long Beach, several network news vans and helicopters were awaiting. The six friends disembarked as a group, gradually separating and integrating into the throng of passengers milling toward the exit. Paige checked her makeup, then artfully changed her direction toward a reporter who was looking back and forth between a campaign picture of Spencer's Magnificent Seven and the arriving passengers. Bastian straightened his collar, by coincidence approaching the same reporter. Palmer, not wanting any exposure, put on a pair of dark sunglasses and plotted a course away from the journalists. As CK led Cassie through the crowd, his eyes trailed Lexa, who was making a retreat toward the open arms of her Uncle Claude, who was fighting his way toward her through a sea of anxious tourists. Claude hugged his shaken niece, then scuttled her to his car through a contingent of reporters clamoring for an interview. When he started the car and drove away, Lexa's spirit plummeted by the sight of the chaos of media scavengers feasting on the carrion of her murdered friend.

***

Claude and his charge arrived at the house. When they pulled into the driveway, Lexa saw her brother and Aunt Amanda waiting impatiently on the porch. When the car came to a complete stop, Alex leapt off the steps and rushed to the passenger side. Lexa threw open the door and jumped out, embracing her twin. As they held each other, Lexa could feel herself drawing restorative energy from Alex, who was intentionally sending it into his distressed sister. For the longest while, the entwined twins' communion made them oblivious to all around them, like two withdrawal-ridden addicts receiving their much needed fix.

Claude closed the trunk, then took the luggage up to the porch where his wife was waiting to greet her niece.

"Is she okay?" Amanda asked her husband. The trepidation in her voice matched the disquiet in her eyes. "How does she seem? Maybe we should—"

"She seems okay, all things considered," Claude answered. After setting down the luggage, he wrapped his arms around Amanda and gave her a kiss on her lips. "What she needs is for us to allow her some space, and some time to process it all." When Amanda opened her mouth to speak, he placed his index finger on her lips. "Okay?"

Amanda sighed in resignation.

After breaking their timeless embrace, Lexa took Alex's hands and asked, "Always?" She looked at him through tear-filled eyes as she placed one of his hands over her heart.

"Always," Alex repeated. "Forever?" he asked, taking Lexa's hand and placing it over his heart.

"Forever," answered Lexa.

Alex pressed Lexa's hand tightly against his chest while giving her a look that shot straight through her eyes and pierced her soul. "Forever isn't long enough," he said. They gazed at each other for another moment or two, then glanced over at their aunt and uncle who were watching them from the porch. "Well I guess we better not keep them waiting any longer."

"Yeah, I guess you're right," Lexa replied.

"I always am," Alex said with a devilish grin. He stretched out his arm toward the porch. "Shall we?"

Lexa took a calming breath and then started toward the porch with Alex following closely behind. The closer she got to the house, the stronger she felt the telltale signs of a massive headache mounting behind her eyes.

Aunt Amanda's self-restraint abandoned her and she rushed off the porch to throw her arms around her niece. "Oh my baby!"

Amanda's smothering clench and excessive blubbering caused Lexa to lose it and weep aloud as well, not just for the loss of her close friend, but also for the stark realization of where she was—a pretty prison she'd been sentenced to since the age of eight, a place where escape seemed impossible.

Other girls her age had experienced middle school and high school, with its homecoming dances and proms, first crushes and first kisses, its cliques to vie for and social strata to navigate—all things Lexa missed out on because of her home-schooling and strict, unsocial upbringing. What of the things possibly yet to come? Career, marriage, house, kids? All things made possible after gaining one's independence. Not that Aunt Amanda and Uncle Claude were monsters. No, just the opposite. They cared too much, to the point their care overwhelmed and suffocated her. Their overprotectiveness was fueled by their desire to see no further havoc wreaked upon her already damaged psyche. And what of Alex? Always and forever? How would one separate a pair so joined at the hip? Was her desire for freedom and a life on her own stronger than her interdependent attachment for her twin? How could she willingly leave someone she couldn't live without? Without her, could Alex even survive? How could she both stay with him always, and leave him to follow her dream to be on her own? She was aware she couldn't do both, and that awareness was slowly sending Lexa teetering toward the edge of sanity...

"Let's get you inside," Aunt Amanda said, shuffling her into the house.

Amanda sat her niece down in the middle of the couch and wrapped her in a throw blanket that she had crocheted. "Now you just relax while I run and get you a hot cup of tea." Aunt Amanda wiped her tear swollen eyes and disappeared into the kitchen.

Uncle Claude walked up to Lexa, kissed the top of her head, and carried her luggage upstairs to her bedroom.

Lexa's and Alex's eyes met and they shared a silent moment of acute mutual understanding in which only twins were able to participate:

Alex: Are you really okay? I would have died if anything happened to you.

Lexa: I'm okay. Well, not really, my head is killing me. I'm just glad to be back with you.

Alex: I missed you, Sis. You are my whole world.

Lexa: I missed you, X-Man. You were in my thoughts the whole time I was away.

Alex: I will always love you.

Lexa: I will forever love you.

The twins were brought back into the world around them by the somber voice of a television news anchor. *"...take you live to the Catalina Landing in downtown Long Beach..."*

"Here we are," Aunt Amanda said, entering the room carrying a steaming bone china cup of tea. "Careful, it's hot." She passed the cup to her less than receptive niece.

"Thank you," Lexa said coldly. She took the cup and set it down upon the coffee table in front of her.

Aunt Amanda painted on a smile, then turned toward the television.

"The victim, Kimberly Clark, was a key member of the newly elected Senator Spencer Storm's campaign team. Surviving members of the team had this to say..."

"Oh my God! That's Paige!" Alex exclaimed when a close-up of her face filled the screen.

Lexa shrank into the couch. On the screen, Paige said, *"I just can't believe what's happened. I mean, who would do something like that to Kimmy? She was..."*

"My God." Lexa turned her pain-ridden head in disgust. *Now, Paige? At a time like this? Can't you go one fucking day without the need to take center stage?*

Lexa's best friend Kimmy was dead—butchered—and the Plastic Princess was up there working a sound bite, the self-centered bitch!

"Maybe this isn't something you should be watching," Amanda said gently.

"You think?" Alex muttered.

Bastian's interview was next: *"I just hope Captain Styles is able to come up with more than..."*

Amanda switched off the television. "There." She glanced at the cup sitting in front of her niece. "You better drink your tea before it gets cold."

"Why?" Lexa snapped.

The attitude caught Amanda off guard. "I beg your pardon?"

"Why should I drink my tea before it gets cold?" Unable to come up with a sensible answer, her aunt is struck speechless. "I mean, is my drinking hot tea gonna bring Kimmy back?"

"Lexa," Alex murmured.

"Or will my drinking hot tea cure all of my psychological issues?"

"Lexa!" Alex hissed.

"Like the inability to cope with the death of my parents?"

"Lexa, that's enough," Uncle Claude shouted from the staircase. He walked over and stood next to his wife, who was on the verge of an emotional deluge. He put his hands on Amanda's shoulders. "Don't take your sorrow and frustration out on your aunt. She's trying her best to help you right now."

"I know," Lexa said apologetically. "I'm sorry."

I'm sorry that drinking water from steeped tea leaves can't bring the dead back to life. I'd be happy if it'd just give me a little relief from this goddamn headache!

Alex gave his sister a knowing look and shook his head.

Alex: No, Lexa. This isn't you.

Lexa cast her eyes downward for a long moment. She snuck a look at the prescription bottles inside her purse and looked back up at her brother.

Lexa: I know it isn't.

A smidgen of alarm hid behind Alex's comforting smile. *Yeah, that outburst was more Alex than Lexa.*

Claude and Amanda looked at each other with concern, then back at their troubled niece.

"Maybe it was a little too soon for you to go away on your own like that," Uncle Claude said.

Lexa whipped her head around to face her uncle with appalled eyes.

"Oh shit," Alex said quietly, sinking down in his seat.

"Too soon?" Lexa snarled. "Too soon for what? Are you trying to tell me that Kimmy was killed because I left home too soon?"

"No. No, sweetheart! I just meant too soon to go off into the world without having your psychological support structure, that being your aunt and I, Dr. Cross...and Alex."

"What does my psychological support structure have to do with Kimmy?"

"Nothing. That's the whole point," Claude said. "It has to do with you and the way you're dealing with her death."

"I'm dealing with it just fine." *This is only making the pain worse. Just leave me alone!*

"Are you really? You're not acting like the same Lexa who left for that damn trip. I'm sure Dr. Cross would say the same."

"What is it that you all want from me?" Lexa yelled. Her hand unconsciously reached into her purse for a medicine bottle. "I've already spent practically my entire life right here inside this house, making it feel more like a prison than a home. For reasons unknown to me, Alex was allowed to get his education like most other kids, while I was sentenced to home school." Lexa took her hand out of her purse to wipe a tear falling down her cheek. "I've missed out on so, so much."

"What are all these things you missed out on?" Uncle Claude asked.

"You want a list? How about playgrounds, field trips, summer camps, sports, dances, friends, birthday parties?"

"That's not true!" Amanda exclaimed in desperate defense of decisions she always thought were right, and ones she was always told were right. "You haven't gone not one year without us celebrating your birthday."

Lexa snorted. "You and Uncle Claude sitting at the table with me and Alex is not my idea of a loads of fun birthday party for a young girl. Oh I forgot, Dr. Cross did manage to make it to my Sweet Sixteen." She picked up the cup of tea and held it aloft. "Here's to the good Dr. James Cross." She slammed the cup down without taking a drink. "I was robbed of a normal childhood because of him, and because of you."

"We just figured that—"

"I wanted so badly to go to school, to be a normal kid like all the ones I used to watch through the window walking to the corner to wait for the school bus. I never was allowed to go. I had to wait until I was old enough to enroll myself, but by that time *school* was freaking *college!*"

"I'm…we're sorry if you suffered because of us in the past," Claude threw out. "But look at you now, graduating with honors, working toward your master's degree, and what about all the new friends you have? Like your Magnificent Seven?"

Lexa scoffed. "Friends? Do you seriously think I know what it means to have a friend, or be someone's friend? I've just been going through the motions. The sad reality is I haven't a clue what real friendship is supposed to be. I have no frame of reference other than what I've seen on TV." She looked over at Alex standing next to the fireplace. "There's only been one person in my life I've ever been able to feel a connection with, one person who sees and knows the real me that's trapped inside of here." Lexa pointed to her head. "And the Magnificent Seven? You wanna know how I feel when I'm around them? I feel like an alien. They only like me because I'm smart and nice to look at. None of them really know me."

For that matter, do I really know myself?

"And anyway, it's not the Magnificent Seven anymore. We're down to six, remember?"

The heart-wrenching feeling of complete and

utter failure ravaged Amanda. Through apologetic eyes, she looked to her niece for some degree of absolution, but none was offered. "We were only doing what we thought was best for you, Lexa. We, all of us, have always done what we thought would make you better."

"Do I *look* better?" Lexa shouted. "Wasn't it bad enough I was an orphan? Why did you have to go and make me a goddamn social retard as well?"

Lexa averted her eyes as her aunt's expression brimmed with telltales she was about to emotionally unravel. After a gut-wrenching moment, Amanda lost the battle and ran weeping into the kitchen.

"You happy now?" Claude asked. He took a deep breath, counting to ten to himself. He had to remain calm and remember that it wasn't her fault. It never was. Claude looked at the ajar kitchen door, then walked over and stood facing his niece. "You know this isn't you, Lexa. This isn't who you really are. Have you been taking your medication as prescribed?"

"Yes," Lexa snapped.

"Really?" Claude motioned to the bag on her lap. "Let me see."

Lexa's hands tightened around the purse's strap. "No."

Alex sighed. "Looks like I'm not needed here." He headed over to stoke the fire.

"No?" Claude repeated. "Why not, Lexa?"

"I'm a twenty-two-year-old woman. An adult capable of keeping account of my own prescriptions."

"Well if that's the case, why don't you just let

me see them?"

"Why don't you just go to Hell?"

"Lexa!" Amanda cried out from the kitchen entryway with shocked disbelief. "What's gotten into you? You've never addressed us in such a manner."

"Yeah, well I've never witnessed a fried human head fall out of a goddamn stock pot either." Lexa got up and headed upstairs. Alex put down the fireplace poker and followed his sister.

***

Lexa crashed down upon her bed with both the sorrow of her loss and the pain from her headache fighting for her attention. She rifled through her purse for her medicine bottles.

Shit…Shit…Shit!

Each bottle she pulled out of her purse was empty.

Watching silently from the hallway, Alex sauntered into Lexa's bedroom. He brushed aside the empty prescription bottles at the foot of her bed and sat down.

"That was so *Twilight Zone* I can't believe it," he said with an air of delight. "It was like I was watching myself have a go at auntie and unkie." He pantomimed boxing moves.

"I don't know what came over me," Lexa confessed. "But whatever it was, I couldn't stop it."

"Don't worry, Sis. It's probably just all your pent-up sexual energy desperately looking for some kind of release. I told you how to take care of that."

Alex laid down on the bed and made a loud buzzing sound, mimicking the moves of a woman pleasuring herself with a vibrator.

"You're an idiot," Lexa said with a girlish giggle. Then she realized that not only had the edge been taken off her headache, but it was starting to lessen in intensity.

"Yeah, well what does that make you, oh twin sister of mine?"

"It makes me the luckiest girl in the world." Lexa embraced her brother tightly. Why was it that him, and only him, could always make her feel better?

Alex grinned. "Headache starting to go away, huh?" Lexa nodded. "Lie down and relax, and I'll go and get your scripts refilled, okay?"

Lexa placed her hand on Alex's cheek and asked, "What would I do without you?"

Alex stroked Lexa's hair thinking, *That's something you'll never have to find out.*

CHAPTER EIGHT

REQUIEM FOR ONE

Dark rain clouds hovered ominously over Holy Cross Cemetery, where old Father McCurtain was commencing Kimber's graveside services. Alex, Lexa, Paige, CK, Cassie, Bastian, and Palmer gazed sadly at their friend's closed casket.

"May her soul, and the souls of all the faithful departed, through the mercy of God, rest in peace. Amen," Father McCurtain ended with grave solemnity, after which he walked over to comfort Kimber's family members.

The friends remained seated while Alex and the rest of the funeral party departed. The sealed casket sat before the six friends like a grim herald of tragedy yet to come.

After allowing them a few minutes to lament, Captain Styles exited her car and approached the group from behind. "Sorry to disturb you at this time, but I said I'd be here." Captain Styles pulled up a chair and sat down.

"Do you have any leads yet on who killed Kimber?" asked Bastian.

"Not one. That's why I'm here today," Styles replied, privately thinking, *So I can do a little more fishing in your ponds.* "By the way," she faced Bastian, her words dripping with sarcasm, "Thanks for your sincere vote of confidence the other day on TV."

"Don't mention it," Bastian replied.

Styles reached into her purse and pulled out Lexa's cellphone and held it out to her. "Thank you for the use of your phone, Ms. Rhodes."

Lexa took it. "Were you able to trace where the texts came from?"

"Yes. Both calls were made from the victim's cellphone and forwarded through a web service called Roommates." Styles honed her attention on Lexa. "You have an awful lot of received and forwarded messages from that site."

"That's just a social network that we all belong to," CK explained. "It's the most popular—"

Captain Styles raised her hand to shush CK. "You seem to have a habit of answering for Ms. Rhodes, in a protective kind of way. Are you two boyfriend/girlfriend?"

CK lowered his eyes. "No, just good friends."

"Then I guess you won't mind if she answers my questions for herself, huh?" Styles took a notepad and pen out of her smart looking, but slightly worn attaché case. "You've all had time to get over the initial shock. Can any of you think of a reason why this happened to Ms. Clark?"

Lexa and the others remained silent while

looking at one another.

"Did she have any rivals, enemies, jilted lovers…?"

"She was having problems with her ex-boyfriend Doug," Lexa said.

"We checked him out. He's been in county lockup for the past week for aggravated assault and battery." Styles looked from one to the other. "Anyone else?"

No one had anything to offer.

Knowing sometimes silence spoke more than words, Styles said, "There were no signs of forced entry at the apartment, so either the killer was someone the deceased knew, or the killer had a key. Ms. Rhodes, do you know of anyone besides the deceased who had a key to the apartment."

"No, no one."

Wait, that's a lie. Kimber gave me a spare key to keep in case of emergencies. But it's hidden in a safe place that no one knows but me. Should I tell her? Alex would say, "Hell no—it might point blame your way, Sis." Maybe he's right. Besides, that's what he would do. But I'm not Alex, I'm me, right?

During Lexa's internal discussion with herself, Styles had been closely watching, trying to unearth any buried secrets the young woman might be struggling to keep covered. She allowed a few moments then prompted, "Miss Rhodes?"

"Yes, Captain Styles?"

"Is there something you want to say?"

No, don't tell her about the key. Kimber wouldn't want you to needlessly incriminate yourself.

79

"No," Lexa said finally. "No, there isn't."

"You see," Styles said, frustrated, "here's my problem. By no means was Ms. Clark's murder random. She was targeted by a sadistic, brutal killer. One who hated her with a passion." She looked over the group. "Do you have any idea how messy it is to kill someone by cutting their throat? Ever hear of arterial spray? Ms. Clark didn't just have her throat cut, someone sawed her head off with a hunting knife." Lexa and Cassie cringed. "So you can imagine how much blood ended up on the killer."

The six friends shut their eyes and grimaced in shared disgust.

"What's the point of you grossing all of us out?" Palmer asked.

"The point is, Mr. Randolph, that Ms. Clark's murder was very personal in nature. Personal enough to use a knife as the murder weapon, forcing the killer to get dead bang close to Ms. Clark. Personal enough for the killer to smuggle Ms. Clark's head over to Catalina Island and then stuff it in a turkey pot." Styles looked directly at Palmer and shook her head. "You can't get much more personal than that." She stood up and opened her attaché. "If any of you remember anything that could help us in our investigation, be sure to give me a call, huh?" She handed each of them her business card. "Thank you all for you time, and my condolences for your friend." Styles turned to leave, then stopped and added, "By the way, why do you think the killer took on all of that trouble and risk ruining your little soiree? The killer first had to successfully transport the head undetected to

Avalon. Then the killer had to slip past the caterers and stow Ms. Clark's head into a boiling pot of peanut oil, and dispose of the turkey that was previously occupying it. After all of that, the killer had to avoid capture after the fact. That much trouble and risk suggests to me that the killer probably has issues with one or more of you, or possibly with the senator himself. In either case, you might want to play it safe for a while. You know, watch each other's backs. I'll let you know if we come up with anything new."

The six watched Styles depart, their minds struggling to fully absorb the relevance of the captain's unsettling warning. After a few moments, Cassie broke the uneasy silence.

"Lexa, are you sure no one else has a key to Kimmy's place?"

"Like Doug perhaps?" Paige added.

"No, she would've told me if she gave him one," Lexa replied with a hint of uncertainty that Paige noticed.

"Are you sure about that?" countered Paige.

Why the hell did Paige ask me that question? I'd know if anyone else had a key, wouldn't I? Unless Kimber didn't tell me. Or someone had a key made without Kimber knowing. Or someone used my key.

"I...I don't know if I'm sure." A familiar pain started building inside Lexa's head, a pain fueled by her self-doubt giving way to self-accusation.

Maybe I used the key. No. I'd never hurt Kimber. What reason could I possibly have? And the way it was done—I could never do anything like that to anyone, let alone my best friend.

She put her hands over her face and wept, her head throbbing with pain.

CK cautiously moved toward Lexa. "Is there something—"

His attempt at consoling her was intercepted by Paige, who leaned over and wrapped her arms around her tearful friend. CK slumped back into his seat.

I sure blew that opportunity. I wonder how many that makes now?

***

Unseen by grieving eyes, somewhere dark, secluded, and hidden from view, a hooded figure watched Paige hug Lexa, talk softly into her ear, and stroke her hair.

CHAPTER NINE

SPIRAL

The pain in Lexa's haunted head was almost unbearable as she walked through the front door. She shut it behind her, securely locking the deadbolt. She strolled over to the chessboard and studied it until the burning wood in the fireplace drew her attention. Her sea green eyes fixed upon orange flames performing a mesmerizing dance in front of a stage of blackened bricks. Once again, Lexa was overcome by the feeling of losing herself.

No. Please, no more.

Lexa struggled to resist, but could not prevent herself from spiraling toward the dead orange flames licking the red bricks...

***

I'm spiraling.

Carl and Lisa Rhodes screamed, thick smoke from the flames choking and blinding them.

83

Please help me! Can't stop spiraling.

Alex dragged his hysterical eight-year-old twin sister from the burning cabin as she screamed for Mommy and Daddy.

I'm spiraling back into oblivion…

***

After everything faded to black, a strong, familiar voice entered the void.

"Lexa, can you hear me? Lexa, wake up…"

Lexa opened her eyes. Dr. James Cross, now in his mid-fifties, was standing over her. Ever since the death of her parents, Cross had been Lexa's treating psychiatrist and her primary care provider.

"There you are," he said with a strong but soothing voice. "Nice to have you back with us."

"Dr. Cross…what happened?" asked Lexa.

Am I awake, or am I asleep? And is there a difference between the two?

"You tell me," Cross countered. "I thought I'd drop by to see how you were doing." He picked Lexa up off the floor and cradled her in his arms. "I rang the doorbell several times, but there was no answer." Cross gently placed Lexa upon the couch. "The front door was ajar, so I peeked inside and saw you lying on the floor." He walked back over to the fireplace and picked up her purse from the floor.

Dazed and confused, Lexa tried to fill in the blanks. "But I…I thought I closed…"

"I beg your pardon?" asked Cross, handing her the purse.

"Nothing."

"I better check you out." Dr. Cross reached for his brown leather physician's bag, the kind you'd expect to see in an old black-and-white movie. After a quick examination, he closed his bag and patted Lexa's knee. "You seem okay physically. So talk to me, what's going on in that head of yours?"

Why should I have to tell him? After all these years he should already know.

"My headaches are getting worse," Lexa confessed. "They're more frequent and intense than ever before."

"Are you taking your prescriptions as I've directed?" His young patient gestured compliance. Cross folded his arms. "That's not what your uncle thinks."

Orange flames erupt behind Lexa's sea green eyes. "Yeah, well I don't give a damn what he thinks."

Maybe I don't give a damn what you think anymore either.

"He told me what happened the other day, the day you arrived back home."

"Really? What a surprise. And?"

Sensing he was probing a raw nerve, Dr. Cross changed gears. "I know you're still having trouble dealing with long repressed memories of your parents' deaths, and how their deaths irrevocably affected your childhood. I also know you've been through hell trying to deal with your friend Kimberly's murder. One can sympathize with all of that, and I do. But none of that justifies taking higher and more frequent doses of your medicines than I have prescribed." Cross reached over and pulled out an empty prescription bottle from Lexa's purse. "If you don't follow my instructions, your pills can do more harm than good."

"I know," Lexa conceded, "but the pills don't even take the edge off the pain anymore. And I'm..." She hesitated.

Should I tell him? What will he do if he knows?

"...I'm starting to have flashbacks again. Of the cabin," Lexa admitted. "They're getting stronger and more vivid each time."

Cross looked down toward his shoes—brown Berluti Oxfords that precisely matched the color of his bag. "Kimberly's death is probably the reason for your aggravated headaches."

"No, they got worse right before I left for Avalon."

"Tell me about your flashbacks," Cross said, still staring at his impeccably polished shoes.

"They started just after I left for Avalon."

"Were you experiencing any added stress at that time?"

"I was upset. I hated having to be away from Alex for Thanksgiving. He looked so sad and alone when I left that morning."

Dr. Cross sat quietly for a moment, staring at Lexa.

Lexa tried matching Cross's stare, but was only able to return timid glances.

"Maybe I was wrong," said Cross. "Maybe you weren't ready to go out on your own like this yet."

Lexa struggled to keep her composure.

I knew you'd say that, you asshole.

Cross opened his journal and took out his pen.

86

"I'm increasing your dosage to help you deal with the headaches. And remember, absolutely no alcohol is ever to be taken along with any of your prescriptions." He tore off a fresh prescription and handed it to Lexa, but kept his grip upon it after she touched it, his stare piercing deep into her green eyes. "We never meant to hurt you, Lexa, or make you feel like a prisoner." Lexa turned away for a few seconds, then back toward the doctor. "There's a lot that you don't remember about those years." Dr. Cross clasped his free hand over the new prescription they were both holding. "What was done was done for your own protection." He released his grasp on the prescription.

Lexa stuffed the new prescription into her purse. "Thank you, Doctor," she said.

No—fuck you doctor!

"You're welcome. And remember, no appointment necessary. My door's always open for you."

Lexa showed Dr. Cross to the door.

"Never forget what John Donne taught us," he said from the porch. "We are not islands to ourselves. We're all here to help each other. Sometimes the only way to receive that help is to reach out for it." Cross winked and then left.

Lexa shut the door and hurried upstairs to her room.

Slamming the door behind her, she rushed to her desk and grabbed a framed picture of herself and Kimber.

Please God, let it be here.

Lexa removed the easeled backing and found a

key labeled "Kimber" taped behind the picture. She breathed a sigh of relief while replacing the backing, then sat down in her chair and tearfully stared at the picture of her and her dead friend.

CHAPTER TEN

LESSON LEARNED

CK stood behind a lecture hall podium teaching Professor Riggins' Psychology 101 class. A third of the students vigorously took notes and hung on every word spoken by the handsome grad student. The other two-thirds whiled away the time with everything from doing their makeup to posting selfies on their Roommates page.

"Obsession is a narrow scope held up in front of the mind's eye that focuses attention on one thing, and one thing only. Like all other addictions, it gives its user, or more accurately its host, a euphoria unequaled to anything else they've previously experienced. Unfortunately, as time goes by, the lives of those obsessed become unbalanced, as all their time and energy is spent desperately trying to recapture the pure ecstasy of that first obsessive high. If left unchecked and untreated, obsession can grow and evolve into what some would diagnose as a psychosis. This condition may lead those plagued by it to engage in activities such as harassment, stalking, and even murder."

A girl in the first row raised her hand. "Like in that movie *Fatal Attraction*?"

"Exactly," CK said. "Obsessions start innocently, but often evolve into what some in the psychological community would classify as a mental disorder." CK pressed a button on the podium and a projection screen lowered in front of the chalkboard. "Someone get the lights, please." As the lights went down, so did the noise. He picked up a slide projector controller and advanced the first frame. The cell phone in his shirt pocket started to vibrate. He snuck his phone out and saw Lexa's picture on the screen.

Seriously? You pick now to call?

He pushed "accept" and whispered into the mouthpiece, "Hello?"

"Hi, CK, it's Lexa. Gotta a free minute or two?"

CK looked around the packed lecture hall in front of him. "Uh, sure. Sure I do."

"Great."

"Just gimme a second and I'll be right back, okay?"

"No prob."

CK thought for a moment, looking around the darkened classroom until his eyes found the girl in the front row who'd asked him the question. He caught her attention and motioned for her to come forward. When she reached the podium, CK said, "Do me a favor. Wait thirty seconds, and then advance the frame until you reach the last one, okay?

"Sure," she said. "Sounds easy enough."

90

"Thank you." After handing her the remote for the projector, CK hurried to the back of the room near one end of the chalkboard. "So what's up?" he said into the phone.

"Nothing much, just following John Donne's advice."

"John Donne?"

"I mean I just wanted to talk."

"Sure. Hey, I'm always c-cool w-with—I m-m-m…I mean I'm d-d-down with…"

Take a breath and stop stammering, you fucking idiot!

"What I'm trying to say is that I'm always here for you if you wanna talk, or something."

Oh that was way cooler, dude. Yeah, right.

"Thanks, CK."

"You're very welcome."

After several moments of silence passed, Lexa said, *"I just…I still can't believe what happened to Kimber."*

"Yeah, me either."

"I…um…"

"What?" CK prodded.

"Nothing."

"That doesn't sound like nothing, Lexa. Go on, tell me."

"It's just that…I don't want to sound self-centered, but I can't stop thinking what if I was there when…when it happened."

"That's not being self-centered," CK told her.

"Then what am I being?"

"I dunno, normal, I guess. I'll tell you this, if I was you, I'd be thinking the same thing right now."

"Really? Guess I'm not as awful as I thought."

"No, don't worry, you're not."

I don't think you're awful at all. In fact, I think you're quite the opposite. I think you're wonderful. The most wonderful, beautiful, intelligent, sexy woman I've ever seen. Too bad I haven't the guts to tell you all of that out loud.

"Who could do that to Kimber? And do what they did on the island?" CK offered no response. *"Do you think the police will ever catch him?"*

"Who knows?" CK replied. "But I hope they do though, and soon. Someone who would do something like that shouldn't be walking the streets. He should be..." The image of the hooded chef from Storm's Thanksgiving party popped into CK's head. "I did see someone, at the Thanksgiving feast. A guy in a chef's uniform wearing a hood over his face."

"You saw him?" Lexa asked excitedly. *"I saw him too, the same guy!"* A wave of fear washed over her. *"He was standing across the pool. Just standing there, staring at me."*

"Yeah, that's what he was doing to me. I think he was holding something too, a bag or something."

"Do you think he was the killer?"

"I dunno. All I do know is he was weird and out of place."

Lexa sighed. Weird and out of place was the story of her life. *"I told the FBI about him, but they didn't seem too interested. Captain Styles hasn't mentioned him at all."*

"Yeah, yeah, I know." Nervous perspiration made it difficult for CK to keep his grip on his cell phone.

C'mon, CK, man up and finally tell this woman how you feel.

"Lexa…"

"Yes?"

"I just want you to know…" He struggled to speak his heart, but as usual nothing was coming out.

"Know what?" Lexa asked with girlish curiosity.

"I just…"

Go on, you pussy, don't stop now!

"I just want you to know that if you ever need to talk, or just hang out or something, my door's always open. If it's not, I keep a key inside the flower pot next to the window."

What the fuck was that? What happened to telling her how I feel about her? What happened to telling her how much I want her? What happened to—

"Aw, that's so sweet, CK. Thank you."

Goddamn great. Now he'd sunk down into the "sweet" category. The bright, blank screen signaled to CK that the slide presentation had just ended. The female student at the podium shrugged and held up the remote control to the projector. "Um, I'm sorry, Lexa, but I gotta go."

"Oh, okay," Lexa said. *"Um, I just want to thank you."*

"For what?"

"For being here for me. And for being a good friend."

CK cringed in the darkened room. "Don't mention it."

Yeah really, don't. Friend?

He had to do something about this, and fast, or he'd never be able to crawl out of the "friend" sinkhole.

"Okay, I'll see ya later."

"Okay."

Yeah—you will.

"Bye, CK."

"Bye." CK hung up, stuck his phone into his pocket, and headed toward the podium.

Another missed opportunity. I guess the old adage is right. "He who hesitates is lost." Well the next time I get the chance, I'm sure as hell gonna take it.

CHAPTER ELEVEN

THE PIKE

The Pike at the Rainbow Harbor was the name of a waterfront entertainment district in downtown Long Beach. With over three hundred and fifty square feet of places to go and things to do, the Pike was one of the city's most popular places to shop, eat, and have a good time. There was even a giant Ferris wheel. What more could one ask for?

Paige, Cassie, Bastian, and Palmer sat in their usual outdoor table of Rob's Joint, a vintage hipster restaurant/bar along the Pike. Cassie scanned one of the menus with her mobile phone's KNFB Reader. The state of the art text-to-speech software was the newest addition to her arsenal of assistive devices. The reader's computerized female voice read aloud: *"Turkey club sandwich, turkey wrap, spicy turkey burger, turkey with—"*

"Jesus, Cass, would you move to another part of the menu please?" Bastian groused.

"Sorry." Cassie turned off her K-Reader and put

it away.

"I never want to see another turkey again," Palmer said. He glanced about the restaurant. "Aren't Lexa and CK coming?"

"Nope," Bastian answered. "CK's teaching a class for Professor Riggins and I think Lexa's off somewhere crying to her shrink."

A waitress who was dressed like a refugee from the Age of Aquarius walked up to their table. "Do you wish to order now?" she asked with little enthusiasm.

Cassie turned toward the sound of the waitress's voice. "Yes, please. I would like—"

"Just freshen up our coffees," Bastian interrupted in his trademark insolent fashion that had earned him the nickname "The Bastard" among his peers.

"Yes sir," replied the waitress with more than a hint of sarcasm. She headed for the counter, the fringes on her suede vest swinging to and fro.

Paige glared at Bastian. "Was that really necessary?"

"What?"

"Maybe Cass was hungry."

"It's okay," Cassie said.

The waitress returned with a full pot of coffee. She topped off everyone's cup, all the while sporting a look on her face as if her headband was tied too tight, and left in a huff.

"Look, I didn't invite you guys here to eat," Bastian said with an irritated loudness.

"Then why are we here?" asked Paige, adjusting the silk scarf draped around her neck.

"We're here, Paige, because some fucking

psycho chopped off Kimberly's head and cooked it up for Thanksgiving dinner," Bastian said with such carelessness that it caused Cassie to knock over her cup of coffee. "And I'm not going to rest until we nail the fuck."

Palmer leaned over and helped Cassie with her mess. "I know how you feel, dude, but trying to catch this guy is way, way out of our league. The police and the FBI—"

"Don't know shit," Bastian snapped. "And they probably never will." He took a sip of coffee and put on his best serious face. "It's up to us. We have to do something."

"What can *we* do?" asked Cassie.

Bastian cleared his throat, his usual indicator that he was about to say something very, very important. "We can start by—"

Paige's smartphone's message alert chimed. "One sec." She took her phone out of her purse and read the screen notification:

FORWARDED MESSAGE FROM ROOMMATES: Paige, I'm in town for the weekend. The paparazzi have been on me but I gave them the slip. Meet me on the Queensbay Bridge at 7:00. I can't wait to get my hands on you.—SSS

Paige grinned. She put her phone away, took out her compact, and touched up her face.

"Sounds like someone has a date," Cassie said with utmost certainty.

Paige gave her blind friend a puzzled look. "How did you know that?"

"By the way you were breathing while reading the text, by your opening your compact right after reading the text, by the urgent and hurried way you applied your makeup," Cassie said with a wily grin. "Need I go on?"

"No, I get the picture." Paige stood and slung her purse over her shoulder.

Bastian flashed Paige a look like she just spit in his coffee. "Hold on a sec, we're not finished here."

"We'll finish this another time, when Lexa and CK can make it as well."

Bastian shook his head. "Life does go on, doesn't it? Glad to see all of this hasn't damaged your fuckin' libido."

"How dare you judge me!" Paige exclaimed. "I miss Kimber just as much as you do, probably more, but we can't cry forever."

"We can't cry forever? How fucking profound, Paige. I hope we'd all be holding up that well if it was your fried head in the turkey pot instead of Kimmy's."

"Fuck you, Sebastian!" Paige shouted, realizing she was on the verge of causing an unladylike scene and quickly composing herself. She corrected her posture, tilting her head toward Cassie and Palmer. "Later, guys."

With an exaggerated effort not to catch any further sight of Bastian, Paige left the outdoor dining area.

After a few moments, Palmer said to Bastian in a condemning voice, "That was really uncalled for."

Bastian took a sip of coffee. "Yeah, maybe it was."

***

While on her way to the Queensbay Bridge, Paige noticed a group of small children fussing amongst themselves near the Ferris wheel. As she got closer, she started to realize what was going on. A little girl, dressed in old and tattered clothes, was being picked on by the other children. The little girl's mother, who was selling homemade jewelry from out of a bike cart, could only watch the events unfold. Paige stopped for a moment and watched the little girl sit down in defeat upon the pavement, crying, while the other children surrounded and taunted her.

Those mean little fucks.

Paige headed straight for the helpless little girl and yelled, "Leave her the fuck alone!" Everyone within earshot stopped dead in their tracks, including the children doing the teasing. After parting the circle of mean children, Paige knelt down next to the crying little girl. With a welcoming smile on her face, she stroked the little girl's unwashed hair. The little girl unburied her face from her hands and looked up at Paige.

"Hello, sweetheart. My name's Paige. What's yours?

"Ma…Mary," the little girl said shyly.

"Mary. What a beautiful name for a beautiful little girl." Paige glanced at the children surrounding them. "Mary, would you do me a favor?" Mary nodded shyly. "Good. Now I want you to cover your ears tight, and keep them covered until I tell you to stop, okay?" Mary mouthed "Okay" and put both hands over her ears.

Paige stood up and one by one shot the other children a look that could only be described as wrath personified. That look alone caused the children to take a couple of steps back. "I'm going to say this once, and only once," Paige said. "If I ever, *ever* see one of you repulsive little fucks picking on Mary again, I will pay a gang of lowlifes to find you and kill you and your whole goddamn family." The ring of children backed up and readied for flight. "Now get the fuck out of here!" Paige's words sent the pack of mean children fleeing, screaming for their lives. After a few moments, she looked at Mary and signaled for her to remove her hands from her ears. Mary's mother, who had been watching this whole time, waved at Paige, who waved back.

Paige walked Mary over to her mother, who with a heavy accent said, "Thank you. Thank you."

Paige smiled as she looked down and saw Mary eyeing her silk scarf. She bent down and asked, "Do you like my scarf?" The little girl reached up to touch it. When Mary's mother started to object, Paige politely stopped her. "Well you know what?" She took off her scarf and wrapped it around Mary. "It's yours now." Mary's eyes lit up and she beamed brightly. Paige bent down close to the smiling child. "Just promise me one thing, Mary. Promise me you'll remember that it's not what we wear on the outside that makes us pretty." Paige pointed to Mary's heart. "It's what we have on the inside that makes us pretty."

A tear ran down the mother's face. She motioned to her cart. "Take one. Take one. Is free for you."

Paige looked over the jewelry. She pointed to a beautiful white magnesite braided leather bracelet. Mary's mother handed the bracelet to Paige, who promptly placed it on her wrist. They exchanged unspoken words of appreciation—from the mother for receiving the gift and from Paige for accepting the gift—then turned and saw Mary looking up at the spinning Ferris wheel.

Paige walked over to Mary. "Looks like fun, doesn't it?" she said. Mary grinned. "Have you ever been on it?"

Mary shook her head. "No."

"Well there's no time like the present." Paige pulled two admission tickets for the ride from her purse. "These have been burning a hole in my pocketbook for months now." She held up the tickets.

"There's two of them," said Mary. "Can you come on the ride with me?"

"I can't, Mary. I just ate, and I don't want to take a chance on getting sick." Paige looked at Mary's mother. "Hey, I've got an idea." She led Mary back over to her mother and said, "Why don't the two of you go?"

The mother shook her head while pointing to the cart. "No. No."

Paige took hold of the mother's hand. "It's all right. I'll stand here and watch the cart for you."

The mother looked down at her daughter, who

begged, "Please, Mommy, come with me."

The mother bowed, taking the tickets from Paige's hand. "Thank you. Very much."

"You're very welcome," Paige said. "Now go have a good time with your daughter, and I'll watch over your jewelry for you."

"Okay." The mother took her daughter by the hand and led her toward the Ferris wheel.

That good deed should cover me for a while.

The smirk on Paige's face slowly grew into one crammed with conceit. "So you can't wait to get your hands on me, huh?" she whispered aloud. "Well who could blame you?" She glanced at the Queensbay Bridge in the near distance.

Hold on, Senator. Paige is coming.

CHAPTER TWELVE

PAIGE

Girlish daydreams of a Cinderella-type wedding and A-list parties in the Senator's mansion filled Paige's head as she walked along the sidewalk of the Queensbay Bridge.

Paige Storm. Mrs. Paige Storm. The Senator's wife, Mrs. Paige Storm...

Gradually the chime of her smartphone pulled her back to the world that knew her as Paige Turner. She took out her phone and read the screen:

IM from Roommates: SSS: Is that you?

Paige grinned and looked toward the middle of the bridge where a lone figure was standing in the distance holding a bouquet of yellow roses.

PAIGE: Maybe. Are those for me?

SSS: Yes. And there's a surprise for you inside.

Paige drew closer to the figure and typed:

What kind of surprise is it?

SSS: The kind you wear around your neck.

Damn. Next time it better be a ring, after you serve Melissa with divorce papers, that is.

With the erotic coyness of a stripper wearing a nun's outfit, Paige approached the figure, whose face was shielded from view by the eye-catching bouquet.

"Can't wait to get your hands on me, huh?" she asked, hugging the figure warmly. "Well then," she said, moving the bouquet to reveal the silhouette of a hooded figure, "prove it." Paige stepped up close for a kiss, quickly pulling away with a look of bewildered recognition. "You. Is this your idea of a joke?"

The spark of an electric charge ignited from behind the bouquet, and Paige saw a noose dangling by the figure's side.

"What the fu—"

The hooded figure violently thrusted a stun gun into her open mouth.

***

A Harbor Cruises ship approached the Queensbay Bridge on its way to the *Queen Mary*. A badly dressed male tourist and his female companion stood together on the observation deck as the ship was about to pass underneath the

Queensbay Bridge. The tourist couple oohed and aahed as they gazed up at the bridge's colorful lights.

"Oh, how pretty," the female tourist remarked. "Get some pictures of those lights."

"Okay, hun," said the male tourist. While he fumbled with his newly purchased digital camera, a white magnesite, braided leather bracelet struck him square on the head. "Ow! What the blazes?"

The female tourist rushed over to check on him. "Are you—"

She didn't get a chance to finish her question, because when she looked up she screamed as Paige's lifeless body plummeted from the bridge and jerked to a stop several feet above the ship's observation deck, swaying to and fro as it hung from the noose tied to the bridge's rail.

The male tourist aimed his camera upward and framed Paige in the view finder.

***

The hooded figure sat in a filthy, dimly lit room. There was just enough light to barely make out several cutout photographs of Lexa strewn all over the top of the equally filthy desk.

Lexa's Roommates page's friends list was displayed on the crud-covered monitor, whose skull cursor moved over and stopped on Paige's picture, the number two spot on the list. The word "UPLOAD" appeared on-screen. A click of the mouse replaced Paige's beautiful profile picture with one of a bird's-eye view of her hanging dead from the Queensbay Bridge.

***

A newspaper article ran with a picture of Paige hanging from the Queensbay Bridge with the headline: *Woman Found Hanging From Queensbay Bridge*.

"Goddammit!" Terrence Simms slammed the newspaper on his desk and rapidly started thumbing through his Rolodex.

***

Alex was lying on his sister's bed watching Marilyn Manson's *No Reflection* video on her laptop. Lexa sat at her desk thumbing through a photo album. The remorse-filled tears running down her face splashed down on the photo album Kimberly made for her and her best friend to share.

When Alex looked over and saw Lexa wipe tears from her face, his eyes automatically watered as if it was mandatory for him to share his sister's grief.

"Kimber wouldn't want you sitting here crying like this," he said.

"Please, Alex, not now," said Lexa. "You don't know what it's like to lose a best friend."

"I know how I'd feel if I lost you. I'd rather be dead. I *would* be dead." Alex sat up and faced his sister. "Promise me that we'll always be together," he said desperately.

Her brother's request forced Lexa to face her

dreaded indecision.

Is it time? Should I try and cut the cord? If I do, what will become of Alex?

"Promise me," Alex begged.

Lexa felt her brother's anguish for her to stay overwhelmingly mix with her own anguish of not being able to leave.

"X-Man...I—" was all she could get out before being interrupted by the ringing of her phone. "Turn that down a little."

Alex lowered the laptop's volume and Lexa answered her phone.

"Hello?"

"What the hell's going on?" Simms's voice blasted through the earpiece.

"Uh, Mr. Simms...?"

The bedroom door burst open and Aunt Amanda and Uncle Claude rushed in.

"What's wrong?" asked Lexa.

Amanda, white as a ghost and clutching a newspaper, glanced at her husband before turning back to her niece. "Oh, honey, I'm so sorry. It's Paige..."

Lexa saw the newspaper headline and the picture below. She dropped her phone and fell to her knees weeping as Simms yelled out from the phone, *"Are you there? Lexa? Lexa! Are you still there?"*

Amanda and Claude knelt down and put their arms around their devastated niece while Alex watched helplessly from the bed.

CHAPTER THIRTEEN

DAMAGE CONTROL

Angels Gate Park was where the Magnificent Seven had always gathered to rest, relax, and reflect while downing a couple of six packs. Today the five remaining members were there to mourn. They sat drinking in quiet solemnity on the steps of the stone pavilion that housed the Korean Bell of Friendship, the park's central attraction.

CK threw a newspaper down on the ground. "Paige would never commit suicide," he said.

Bastian took a sip of his beer. "That's what I told Styles."

"You talked to Styles?" asked Lexa. "When?"

"This morning. Palmer and Cassie talked to her too."

"She paid us all a visit earlier because we were the last ones to see Paige alive last night," Palmer explained.

"Well, not the last one," said Bastian. He shook his head and took another drink.

Lexa closed her eyes and placed her hands on her

forehead in an effort to soothe her building headache. "What if she was murdered, like Kimber?" A moment of uncomfortable silence followed. "What are the police going to do to protect the rest of us?"

"Nothing," Bastian snarled. "I asked Styles what steps the police would take if there was a connection between Paige and Kimber's deaths, what steps she'd take to protect what's left of us." He finished his beer, got another, and opened it. "The bitch told me that Long Beach Police Department can't provide round-the-clock security for every citizen who might be in need." Bastian took another swig. "She said just to call her if anything else happens."

"So what happened yesterday at Rob's?" CK looked from Palmer to Cassie and back again.

"We were sitting down talking when Paige got a text message and all of a sudden she got up and left," Cassie answered.

"Did she say who it was from?" asked Lexa.

Cassie shook her head. "No."

"Did the cops check her phone?" Palmer took his personally engraved Zippo lighter from his pocket and nervously polished it with an initialed handkerchief.

"They said she didn't have it on her," said Cassie.

Bastian took out a cigarette. "Betcha it was from Storm," he said, reaching over and snatching Palmer's lighter from out of his hand.

"What was?" asked Cassie.

"The text she got before she ran out of Rob's."

He deftly flipped open the lid of Palmer's Zippo.

Palmer glared at Bastian. How dare he touch his sterling silver lighter?

"What makes you think that?" asked Lexa.

Bastian lit his cigarette and took a deep drag from it, then flipped the lighter closed and tossed it back to Palmer. "Forget it."

"What about Storm?" Palmer pressed, using his handkerchief to wipe Bastian's fingerprints from his lighter. "You think he still wants us on his staff?"

"I'm pretty sure he does," said Lexa. "Simms told me not to worry and that everything should be fine once all of the negative press goes away."

"Negative press?" Bastian echoed. "Oh, you mean Kimber and Paige."

"I'm just telling you what he said." Lexa took a pill from her purse, put it in her mouth, and snatched Bastian's beer out of his hand. She took a healthy swig and then handed him back the bottle.

"So what should we do until then?" asked Cassie.

"Maybe we should all lay low for a while," Palmer suggested. "Play it safe."

Bastian snorted a derisive laugh. "Yeah? Well where's safe?"

"How about my place?" offered Palmer. "We have security up the ass. Surveillance cameras, motion detectors, even a panic room. Besides, my parents are still out of town and I don't want to be alone. How about it?"

Palmer glanced at Lexa. "You game?"

"She's seeing her shrink later," CK said.

Bastian turned a questioning eye toward CK.

"Yeah. After that I'm going to go home and call it a night," said Lexa.

"What about tomorrow?" asked Palmer.

"She has a chess match tomorrow night," CK replied.

Bastian leaned over to Lexa and whispered, "Does he pick up your laundry, too?"

Palmer shrugged. "How about you, CK? Wanna spend the night with me, no strings attached? Well, not unless you want them to be." He gave CK a come-hither wink.

CK laughed. "Thanks for the invite, but I'm going to be on campus grading papers for Riggins all weekend."

"Cass?" Palmer prompted with a sense of desperation.

"Sorry, I have to work on my thesis."

Palmer went next to Bastian. "What about you, handsome?"

"No thanks. Besides, aren't you having Double D's over this weekend?"

"Yeah, so?"

"Who's Double D's?" asked CK.

Bastian snickered. "Delia Denton, a freshman who just made it into Pi Delta Pi."

"Okay, I get it. Double D's stands for her initials," CK said.

Palmer and Bastian looked at each other, smirked, and simultaneously shook their heads and chorused, "Nope."

Cassie giggled. "Sounds like a real sick chick."

"You don't know the half of it," Palmer said.

Lexa picked up her purse and set off for her car.

"I'll see you guys later."

"Guess I upset Miss Chaste Below the Waist," Bastian said.

An instinctual protective rage erupted behind CK's eyes. "Why don't you shut the fuck up?" he said to Bastian. He took Cassie by the hand. "Come on, Cass, let's go." He guided her down the hill toward his car.

"Bye, guys," said Cassie.

"Later," Palmer said.

"Yeah," Bastian chimed in. "See ya."

When the others had gone, Palmer asked Bastian, "Are you serious?" with genuine surprise. "Lexa's a virgin?"

"You ever been in her pants?"

"I've never been inside her house, let alone her pants." Palmer looked toward the parking area. "You think CK's got a hard-on for her?"

Bastian snickered. "Where've *you* been?"

"Mmmm, Lexa. Man, I bet you anything she's a freak in bed."

"The shy ones usually are," said Bastian, raising up his beer bottle. "To freaks."

Palmer raised his beer bottle and clinked it against Bastian's.

***

Lurking unnoticed behind the seventeen-ton Bell of Friendship, the hooded figure watched and waited.

***

Lexa stood gazing at the flames in the fireplace of Dr. Cross's home office.

"Paige was too full of life, and full of herself, to commit suicide. Besides, there wasn't any reason for her to kill herself."

"Maybe she did have a reason," Cross suggested matter-of-factly, "some secret she kept to herself." He studied the chessboard perched near the edge of his desk.

How dare you think you know my friends better than I do?

"No, you don't know Paige. I mean, didn't know. She couldn't keep a secret to save her life." Lexa bent down and stoked the burning wood. "Besides, even if she had wanted to commit suicide, she would never have hung herself."

Cross finally made a move, one that threatened Lexa's queen. "Why not?" he asked.

"Because it's not ladylike, and one thing Paige went out of her way to be was a lady." Lexa stared into the flames.

They're still burning, Alex! Mommy and Daddy are burning in my mind and I don't know if they'll ever stop.

"You didn't like it much the other day when I suggested you weren't ready to go out on your own yet. Did you?"

"No, I didn't." Lexa looked away from the flames, briefly studied the chessboard, and deftly moved her queen out of danger. "Your move, Doctor."

"So it is."

With a grin, Lexa watched her doctor sit in contemplation, strategizing his next move. With his eyes still locked on the chessboard, Dr. Cross said, "Maybe it is time."

"Time for what?"

"Time you go out into the world alone." Cross looked up into Lexa's questioning eyes. "That is what you want, isn't it?"

Of course it is. Isn't it?

"Yes, of course it is." Even to herself, Lexa's words were soaked with doubt.

"It is?" Cross stared down at the chessboard. "Are you trying to convince me, or yourself?"

Several moments ticked by in silence.

Who am I trying to convince? I cannot go out into the world alone without breaking my promise to Alex and I can't keep my promise and go out into the world alone. We can't be together and apart at the same time.

The stark realization of her predicament swept her away like a tsunami.

Always and forever. Were those words just a childish saying, or were they an eternal vow evermore uniting us?

Lexa's mind felt in danger of being sucked into the black hole center of the spiral that had haunted her soul since the death of her parents.

No, I've never lied. I've meant those words. Each and every time I spoke them, I've meant them. I've meant them with all my being.

Lexa was about to speak, but lowered her head in defeat after glimpsing the probing eyes of her doctor. Unseen by her, Cross moved his bishop and took her queen.

Sensing his patient was drowning in a sea of indecision, Cross decided to throw her a life preserver. "You know, a wise man once said that the definition of Hell is getting what you've always wanted."

That's it exactly. Someone else does get it.

"Life doesn't always have to be either/or, Lexa. Often we have to find a way to meet in the middle in order to survive." Cross's fingers stroked Lexa's queen. "Maybe together we can find that happy medium, a quid pro quo that will satisfy both of your desires. Are you willing to try?"

Lexa signaled obedience.

"Good girl." Cross turned the monitor on his desk so that it faced Lexa.

"God, not again," Lexa said. "I hate that thing."

"That's a conundrum I've never come close to solving," Cross said. "Why we seem to always hate the taste of what heals us."

With a few clicks of the mouse the familiar hypnotic animation appeared upon the computer's screen. Lexa stared at the black and white maelstrom in front of her, spiraling down into a sea of nothingness. Still holding the captured chess piece, Cross doused the lights and deepened his voice. "Now, let us begin…"

CHAPTER FOURTEEN

ALEX AND LEXA

Alex sat cross-legged in front of the fireplace, the flames reflecting off his eyes, behind which a maelstrom of emotions exploded out from the darkest recesses of his mind.

Why does she want to leave? She could be in danger. How can I live without her? How can I protect her? Why does she want to leave me? She's my life—I'll let no one come between us. Fuckin' no one…

When Lexa finally arrived home, Alex ran over and wrapped his arms tightly around his sister, holding onto her like grim death.

Don't ever leave me. Don't ever leave me. Don't ever—

"I'm glad to see you too," Lexa said, a wave of uneasiness washing over her while she waited for her brother to release his death grip on her. "Um, did I miss something?"

"I worry about you." Alex released his twin

sister. "You know I do."

"You can stop for the moment. I'm fine."

"Are you?" Alex walked off and headed into the living room.

Lexa closed the front door, took off her coat, and joined Alex, who was standing beside the chessboard.

"What does that mean?" she asked. "Is there something you know that I don't?"

Alex moved a chess piece. "Let's just say that sometimes I have to protect you, from yourself."

Lexa was taken aback by her twin's cryptic remark.

From myself?

"What the hell are you talking about?"

***

Amanda and Claude sat restlessly at the kitchen table eavesdropping on the conversation taking place in the living room.

"Maybe we should keep this for another time," they heard Alex say.

"You started this, so you may as well get it over with," Lexa responded.

***

Alex moved a chess piece. "I don't want you to go to work for that asshole Storm."

"God, Alex, do we have to get into this now?"

"You wanted me to speak my mind, so I am."

Lexa moved a chess piece. "I know you don't want to hear this right now, but Dr. Cross thinks—"

Alex laughed mockingly. "Cross! You think I give a shit what that fuck thinks?" He picked up a chess piece and slammed it down on the board. "I hate that fuckin' prick, and so should you!"

***

Claude put down his newspaper and exhaled a deep sigh of frustration. When he started to get up from the table, Amanda reached over and clutched his arm. "Dr. Cross told us not to interfere," she reminded him. "They'll work out their issues by themselves."

Against his better judgement, Claude conceded to the doctor's orders and sat back down. Dr. Cross knew best, didn't he?

Amanda pushed aside her inner doubt, smiled reassuringly, and caressed her husband's calloused hands.

***

Blind frustration seared Lexa's brain like a red-hot branding iron.

He'll never let me go. I know that now.

"I'm going to my room now. We'll finish this another time."

When his sister turned to leave, Alex gripped her by the arm to stop her. He moved up close behind her and whispered, "Look, some sick fuck's already offed two of your best friends and there's no telling who might be next. I'd die before letting anything bad happen to you."

Lexa gently kissed her brother's hand. "Nothing bad's gonna happen to me, but I am going to work for Senator Storm as soon as I can." Alex frowned and pulled away. "It's my life, Alex," Lexa said. "If I don't start living it, what's the point of having it?" She moved a piece on the chessboard. "Can't you be happy for me? If I were you, I'd at least pretend to be." She took Alex's right hand and placed it over her heart, waiting for her brother to reciprocate.

Alex sighed. He brought up Lexa's right hand and placed it over his heart.

Lexa smiled. "Always and forever." She kissed her twin on his cheek and walked away.

Always and forever? Alex's mood sullied with each leave-taking step Lexa made. His vision narrowed, his eyes zeroing in on his sister climbing the staircase.

Don't you ever say those words to me again, Sis, unless you really mean them.

Alex picked up Lexa's queen and hurled it into the fireplace.

CHAPTER FIFTEEN

PALMER

Palmer and Delia Denton, a buxom eighteen-year-old brunette who looked like the physical incarnation of a men's magazine fold out page, relaxed in a spacious, lighted Jacuzzi. Seductive music played softly through hidden built-in speakers. Between the Jacuzzi and the customized heated pool sat an open laptop, upon which Palmer's Roommates page was displaying on its monitor.

Delia drained her glass of champagne and slid over toward Palmer, who was repeatedly failing his attempts to light his Zippo the way Bastian did the day before. "Are you sure we have the place to ourselves?" she asked.

"No worries. My parents won't be home for another week."

"What about your friends, the Magnanimous Seven?"

Palmer snickered. *Guess you don't need brains*

with tits like those. "They all have other plans."

"How about a brother or sister who's coming home for the weekend?"

"Nope, don't have any."

Delia's interest was piqued. "You're an only child?" she asked with a gold-digging grin.

"As far as I know."

Delia fluffed up her breasts and snuggled closer to Palmer. "So you're your parents' sole heir?"

Palmer bowed in affirmation, setting his Zippo down next to the laptop.

Delia took off her DD-cup size bikini top, draping it around Palmer's neck. "Like what you see?" Before her wide-eyed host could answer, she kissed his lips, her buxom breasts rubbing against his chest. "Mmmm, nice." Delia picked up the champagne bottle and put it upside down into its silver chiller. "Want some more?" she asked Palmer seductively.

"Uh huh." Palmer snapped out of his bosom induced haze. "Oh, champagne. Sure, there's some in the pool house."

Delia kissed Palmer softly and sensuously. "Be right back," she said and climbed out of the Jacuzzi.

***

The Randolphs' pool house resembled more of a luxury condo than simply a place for changing clothes.

Hiding within the grandiose dressing quarters, quietly and patiently waiting in the shadows, the hooded figure watched.

Delia crossed over the threshold into the immodestly decorated pool house. "Well la-di-da," she muttered. Who said money couldn't buy happiness? Once in the kitchen she was awestruck at the elegant custom-made cabinets lining the walls. "So, if I was a bottle of champagne, where would I be?"

The hooded figure stealthily stalked toward the unsuspecting young female strolling barefoot through the kitchen.

Delia opened and closed several cabinet doors before finding the refrigerator. She opened the door and looked inside. The glow from the light gave Delia a surrealistic appearance that inexplicably excited the approaching hooded figure. As she closed the refrigerator door, she had a haunted feeling someone was watching her. Delia whirled around and gazed into the dimness behind her, but saw no one. After sighing with relief, she opened the cabinet door next to the refrigerator to reveal a fully stocked, floor-to-ceiling wine cooler.

"Voilà!"

She looked through the collection, selecting one of the bottles. "Dom Perignon, I guess you'll do." She shut the cabinet door, but before she could turn back around, the hooded figure clamped one hand over her mouth and held up a hunting knife in front of her face with the other.

***

A persistent knocking sound from his Roommates page drew Palmer's attention. He moved his avatar to the peephole and typed:

Who's knocking?

The peephole widened to reveal an avatar of a hooded figure with the screen name IWNTUDED.

Palmer closely examined the screen name. *"I...want...you...de..."* He shook his head and typed:

Bastian, you sick fuck.

IWNTUDED replied:

I am a sick fuck, but I'm not Bastian.

Palmer looked at the computer screen with a sudden sense of anxiety and typed:

Who is this?

IWNTUDED replied:

Someone who thinks you should share the wealth with the less fortunate.

Palmer laughed with relief. *I knew it was you, shithead.*

Okay, Bastian, how much cash do you need this time?

IWNTUDED responded:

I don't want money, and I told you, I'm not Bastian.

Anger trumped Palmer's fear as he typed:

Then who are you and what the fuck do you want?

IWNTUDED typed:

I'm a sick fuck, remember? As for what I want, let's start with the whore in the pool house.

Right when Palmer stood and turned toward the pool house, he heard a beep and looked back at the laptop's screen:

Sit down, or I'll shove my knife into this whore's skull.

Shocked, Palmer slowly sat back down.

Good. Now for your reward. A front row seat.

A live webcam picture opened to reveal Delia bound to a chair with duct tape covering her mouth. The hooded figure held up a stun gun in front of Delia's bosom. A blue electric charge ignited between the two silver contacts, then promptly extinguished.

"You fuck," Palmer breathed.

Delia sat whimpering helplessly while the hooded figure lovingly stroked her hair, slowly circling the stun gun's contacts around one nipple and then the other.

Palmer typed:

NO.

The hooded figure casually pulled the stun gun away from Delia's bosom, then viciously thrust it into the nipple of her left breast.

"No!" Palmer shouted as the stun gun's two million volt discharge sent Delia into unconscious convulsions. He jumped out of the Jacuzzi and raced toward the pool house. On his way, he ripped off one of a pair of decorative wooden oars mounted near the entrance and burst through the pool house door.

Palmer raced into the kitchen and found the hooded figure standing next to Delia, who sat motionless with her left nipple charred and smoldering. Shaking with fear Palmer shouted, "You killed Kimber and Paige, didn't you?"

The hooded figure shrugged "guilty as charged" whilst creeping toward the kitchen sink.

Palmer dug deep inside himself, looking for the adrenaline he needed to bolster his will to fight knowing if he didn't man up, he'd be dead too. He tightened his grip on the oar and defiantly asked, "You wanna kill me too?"

Again the hooded figure gestured confirmation.

Palmer readied his oar for battle and shouted, "Then come on, asshole, kill me!"

The hooded figure reached back and turned the faucet on full blast, pulled out the sink's rinsing hose, then held up the stun gun and shot a stream of water through the electric charge between the contacts. The electrically charged stream of water hit Palmer square in the chest and knocked him unconscious.

***

Palmer Randolph's motionless body laid hogtied on the bottom of the drained Jacuzzi. Several splashes of strong-smelling liquid drew him back toward consciousness.

"Hey…where the…what…" Palmer's reddened eyes began focusing as more of the foul liquid spattered down upon him. "What the fuck?" Managing to roll from off his stomach onto his side, he saw the hooded figure standing at the edge of the Jacuzzi holding something. His eyes strenuously adjusted enough to make out the words "GASOLINE" on the sides of two five-gallon cans.

Oh my God, he's going to fucking burn me!

"No. No, don't!"

The hooded figure doused Palmer with more gasoline from the can.

Palmer desperately tried to inchworm his way up the slippery sides of the gas-filled Jacuzzi, falling and rolling back down to the bottom. With a tearful voice he shouted, "What the fuck do you want!"

Completely ignoring his victim's question, the

hooded figure emptied the last of the gasoline out of the can and tossed it away.

The young man's mind frantically scrambled to devise salvation from the terrible fate he knew awaited him. Everyone loved money, so he'd promise him anything, bribe him!

"My parents are rich and—"

The hooded figure picked up the remaining gas can, opened it, and poured its contents all over Palmer.

"They'll pay you anything you want," Palmer pleaded.

The hooded figure nonchalantly cast the can aside.

"Please, just let me go. I've done nothing to you. I don't even know who you are!"

The hooded figure stood in calm silence for a few moments, holding up Palmer's Zippo.

As the light of the moon glinted off the lighter's high polish finish, a look of anger washes over Palmer's face. "Goddamn you. Goddamn you to Hell!"

The hooded figure snapped the flint wheel to ignite the lighter and threw it into the Jacuzzi.

Palmer erupted into a fiery mass. He screamed and bounced violently about the inside of the Jacuzzi as his hair burned away and his flesh melted and deformed.

Using a smartphone, the hooded figure snapped pictures of Palmer in the eerie light of the flames from the Jacuzzi illuminating the pool area.

Palmer's screams of agony rose above the roar of the flames, diminishing as his body grew still and lifeless.

***

The hooded figure sat in a filthy, half-lit room. Extra lighting now revealed more pictures of Lexa that were taped on the gritty walls. The monitor's skull cursor moved over Palmer's debonair face shot and replaced it with one of his blackened and burnt remains.

CHAPTER SIXTEEN

REALITY IS PERSPECTIVE/PERSPECTIVE IS REALITY

Carrying shopping bags from high-end clothing stores, Lexa and Cassie passed by a restaurant where a waiter served flaming shish kabobs to customers eating alfresco. The anxiety gnawing away at Cassie's psyche made her clutch tightly onto Lexa's arm in a manner very uncharacteristic of her usual self-reliant persona.

What if there was a killer out there who was after the rest of them? She wouldn't even be able to see him coming. What would she do? How could she protect herself?

Her mind split between safely navigating Cassie along the crowded sidewalk and deliberating how to win independence from her overly dependent twin, Lexa accidentally bumped into an aging, overweight man using a walker.

The man lost his balance momentarily, managing to steady himself before he fell. After muttering a masterfully crafted composition of expletives, he glared at Lexa and barked, "Goddammit, you almost knocked me the fuck down!"

"I'm so sorry, sir," Lexa said. "I guess I didn't see you. Are you all right?"

"Didn't see me?" He flamboyantly gestured to his rotund physique. "My ass isn't big enough to catch your attention?" The portly man looked the two young women up and down. Just as he prepared to make another snide remark, he caught sight of the folded white cane dangling from Cassie's wrist. The irony of it all was almost too much for him to acknowledge. He shook his head and muttered, "Talk about the blind leading the blind."

The fat man rudely brushed past Lexa and Cassie, resuming his profane tirade down the sidewalk.

Ill from the verbal molestation, Lexa's knees buckled. She sensed the presence of something far, far worse, the gut-wrenching feeling that preceded the oncome of one of her brain-splitting headaches. She fretfully darted her eyes until they caught sight of a familiar face; her own reflection in one of the storefront windows.

***

Fire had completely engulfed the cabin. When Lexa tried to run back inside, Alex tackled her and held her down on the ground.

"Let me go, Alex, please! Mommy and Daddy are in there!"

They're screaming. They're burning!

130

FRIENDS LIST

***

The fat man incident had also rattled Cassie with chagrin, dredging up all the old feelings of fear and insecurity that took her years to suppress after losing her sight. Forcing a smile, she said, "Lexa, let's find a place to sit down for a minute, okay?" When there was no response, she prompted, "Okay?"

When her friend's prodding snapped her back into reality, Lexa broke eye contact with her mirrored image. "Okay," she said. Still a little emotionally shaky, she led Cassie to a bench where they sat for a while in thought-filled silence.

Cassie had always relied heavily upon her acute hearing and intuitive nature to guide her through her lightless world. Today both of those abilities allowed her to pick up on her friend's inner pain. She reached over and took one of Lexa's hands. "You're going to get through this. We all are," she said with heartfelt empathy.

"I hope you're right." Playing with the locket that dangled from her neck, Lexa thought, *I doubt it, but I can still hope.* "Sometimes I feel like my nightmares are spilling over into reality. I don't know what's real anymore." She leaned down and put her face into her hands.

Is my tortured mind diseased with a Macbethian madness? Is the burning cabin my dagger covered in blood? More importantly, if I were insane, would I even know?

Cassie rubbed Lexa's back in circles. "That's one thing I never have a problem with."

"What's that?"

"Knowing the difference between dreaming and being awake."

"How do you know the difference?"

"When I can see, I know I'm dreaming. And when I can't, I know I'm awake." Cassie blinked away the tears forming in her broken eyes. Why was it that people didn't really appreciate things until they lost them? After a few more moments of doom and gloom, Cassie put her pity party on hold so she could comfort her friend. "I think reality is whatever you want it to be. Happiness, sadness, lovingness, hatefulness..." She squeezed Lexa's hand. "It's all up to you. We're each responsible for creating our own Heaven. Or Hell."

Lexa looked at Cassie with newly gained insight. Maybe it was time she opened her eyes. Looking at her friend, she slowly realized that true vision had nothing to do with your eyes.

A couple sloppily making out on the bench across from them caught Lexa's attention. She started to imagine the kissing couple was her and CK. After a minute of living in her daydream, Lexa decided to seek some more advice from her insightful friend. "Cass?"

"Yeah?"

"Which do you think is worse? Liking someone but never telling them for fear of rejection, or telling someone you like them and getting rejected?"

"By any chance would this person's name happen to begin with a 'C' and end with a 'K'?" A smile spread across Cassie's face. "No worries. Mr. Kane seriously has the hots for you."

"He does?" Lexa asked with surprise. "No way. I so don't believe you. Uh uh, nope."

"Wake up and smell the coffee, girl. Everyone knows. Everyone but you, apparently."

Lexa covered her ears and shook her head while childishly vocalizing, "No, no, no. I don't believe you. No, no, no. I don't believe you. No, no, no. I don't—"

"Okay fine, Lexa. If you don't believe me, then woman-up and ask him yourself." With a baby talk voice Cassie added, "If you want, I'll stand next to you and hold your hand when you do."

Lexa smacked her arm and then they both laughed.

"Anyway, the sooner you find out I'm telling you the truth, the sooner you'll find you and CK doing what those two are doing on the bench across from us."

For the first time in a long time, Lexa laughed a genuine laugh. "Come on you, we better hit the expensive stores. Paige would have a fit if we showed up tomorrow dressed any way other than to the nines."

Unbeknownst to them, the hooded figure eyed Lexa and Cassie from a stealthy vantage point, keenly looking, intently watching.

CHAPTER SEVENTEEN

HEAVEN'S GATES

Banners, flowers, and pictures of the Turners' youngest daughter adorned the entrance of the eighteen-story CSULB Walter Pyramid. Attendance was standing room only, a testament to the deceased's undeniable popularity.

The four members of what was left of the Mag Seven—Lexa, Cassie, CK, and Bastian—sat behind the Turner family. A cluster of slide projectors cast pictures of Paige upon multiple screens inside the darkened pyramid while Corelli's "La Folia" played softly in the background. After generating a plethora of audible tears, some genuine and some contrived, the slide presentation stopped and the lights turned on.

Lexa, Cassie, CK, and Bastian walked to the front of the seating area, one by one quietly paying their respects to the Turners. Afterwards they regrouped near the main exit.

"Hey, where's Palmer?" asked Lexa. "Did any of you hear from him?"

Cassie, CK, and Bastian shook their heads with solemnity appropriate for such a gathering.

Wondering why he wouldn't be there, Lexa noticed Terrence Simms leading Senator Storm toward the Turner family, flanked by half a dozen plainclothes security agents.

"There's Storm." Lexa motioned toward the senator and his entourage.

Bastian glanced at Storm paying his respects to Paige's family. "I'll see you guys later," he said, taking off toward the Senator. As he approached, he was intercepted by Storm's dark sunglasses-wearing security agents.

The lead agent looked the young man up and down and asked, "Is there something I can do for you?"

Who the fuck...don't you know I work for this asshole? Bastian thought.

He shook his head with contempt tainted disbelief. "Yes, you can get out of my way so I can see the senator." He started to move forward, but the agents held their ground and would not let him pass.

Sensing the likelihood of an ugly scene developing, Simms snaked his way through the security staff. "I'm sorry, Bastian, but the senator is running late. He's on a very tight schedule."

"This won't take but a minute." Bastian moved toward the senator again, but two of the agents yanked him back.

"The senator doesn't have a minute," the lead agent stated with firm resolve.

Senator Storm noticed the agents holding a growingly irate Bastian by the arms and shoulders. He caught Simms' attention and motioned toward Bastian.

Simms winked and placed his hand on Bastian's shoulder. "The senator is going to be in town for a couple of days, so why don't we—"

"Look, I just wanna ask the senator a question." Bastian started to move yet again toward the senator and again was swiftly stopped by the security agents.

"You don't want to cause a scene, do you?" asked Simms. "At your friend's memorial service? In front of her parents?"

Bastian glanced at Mr. and Mrs. Turner, back to Simms, and shook his head in persuaded agreement.

"Why don't we find a quiet place where we can talk about your question for the senator?" Simms gestured toward the area behind the projection screens.

Bastian shrugged away from Simms's hand and walked away. Simms followed closely behind.

From the corner of his eye, Storm watched with relief as Bastian and Simms removed themselves from his meet-and-greet zone, the circumference radiating about six to ten feet from its senatorial epicenter, within which salutations and handshakes with the public were mandatory. It was just some more shit that came with the territory of holding a public office. Seeing this as an opportune moment to depart without incident, Storm led his shadowing security toward the main exit where Lexa, CK, and Cassie were standing. He hugged Lexa and Cassie, shook CK's hand, then exited the pyramid.

Lexa spotted Bastian and Simms fussing. The heated argument climaxed with Simms pushing his finger repeatedly into Bastian's chest and hurrying away in a huff toward one of the side exits.

Bastian removed a flask from his pocket and unscrewed the top, noticing Lexa staring at him curiously. He held up his flask toward her in a halfhearted toast, took a healthy swig, and disappeared into the lingering crowd.

CHAPTER EIGHTEEN

CROSS

The offshore breakwaters of the Long Beach Shoreline Marina vigilantly sheltered its host of docked boats. The *RMS Queen Mary*, the renowned ocean liner now turned tourist attraction, appeared just a stone's throw south of the marina.

Walking along the marina's seaward dock deep in thought, Lexa stared blankly at the rippling water. The misty ocean breeze fluttering her mid-thigh skirt was in stark contrast to the violent tempest raging inside her head.

Why does Alex have such hatred for Dr. Cross? All he's ever tried to do is help me. Won't helping me also help both of us?

After passing several moored boats, Lexa headed up a gangplank and climbed aboard Dr. Cross's yacht, *Trilby*. She went onboard and looked around the boat.

"Dr. Cross?" she called out, heading toward the bow. "Dr. Cross?"

As if out of nowhere, Dr. Cross came up behind Lexa with a beer in his hand and an herbal cigarette in the other. "Hi," he said, nearly causing her to jump out of her skin.

She spun around and saw Dr. Cross standing there smiling assuredly at her.

"Sorry, I didn't mean to scare you," he said with a soothingly seasoned voice.

"Dr. Cross, I hope I'm not disturbing you, but you told me that if I ever needed—"

"It's okay, really," Cross assured her. "How did you know I was here?"

"Your secretary told me."

That stupid bitch. He had told his secretary a thousand times that when he was on his boat he was not to be disturbed.

Cross forced a smile. "I'm glad she did. You look like you need to talk."

Lexa nodded with the same anxious affirmation a starving man would show if offered food.

"Shall we have our session on deck?" asked Cross in a spider to the fly intonation.

"Okay." Lexa waited for Cross to lead before following him up to the sun deck.

Dr. Cross finished his beer and sat down. Upon the compass-patterned table in front of him was an open laptop. On the screen was a document titled, *D.I.D. You, or D.I.D. I: The Intricate Nature of Dissociative Identity Disorder" By Dr. James Cross.* He discreetly licked his lips, his eyes sneaking a quick taste of the eye candy standing in front of him. When he saw his young patient eyeing his laptop, he promptly shut it closed. "Please have a seat."

Lexa sat beside Dr. Cross and crossed her legs, waffling with indecision.

Just go ahead and tell him.

She sighed. "I don't like me," she finally managed.

Struggling to keep his eyes from straying toward her tanned, silky thighs, he asked, "Why not?"

"Because I'm so selfish. Even with everything that's happened and is still happening to my friends, and to Alex, all I can think about is leaving them and all of this behind me, that's why."

Cross took a drag from his cigarette and stubbed it out in the Waterford crystal ashtray sitting on the table. "Is that wrong?"

"Yes. It is."

"Why?"

No longer able to hold back the tears fighting to be released, Lexa sobbed, "My best friends are dead, my brother says he'd rather die than live without me, and all I can think of is myself." She wiped the tears from her cheeks.

What the fuck, Doc? Talk about having to spell it out for you.

"Yeah," she said, "I'd call that wrong."

"Maybe," Cross said noncommittally, lighting another cigarette. "But even if it is, what good could you honestly do by staying here?"

Lexa was caught off guard by the simple, blunt question. She paused for a moment, casting her gaze upon the Queensbay Bridge in the near distance. "I don't know. Maybe help find out why Kimber and Paige were killed, and by whom."

Cross shook his head with authoritative contradiction. "That's a job for the police, Lexa, not you."

She took a couple of pills from her purse and swallowed them dry. Maybe he was right.

"How's the new prescription working out?"

"Pretty good," Lexa said. "My headaches have been a little less frequent and severe."

"Good. Glad to hear it." Cross poured her a drink from the iced-filled pitcher sweating on the table. "How about something to wash those pills down?"

"No thank you, I'm fine."

"Don't worry, there's no alcohol in it." Cross pushed the glass toward Lexa, who took it from him.

"Thanks." She took a sip.

Sneaking another lusty peek at Lexa's lovely legs, Cross took a sip of his own drink. "So how's Alex been?" he asked.

"He's been okay." *All things considered.* "He's really been helping me deal with...with what's happened."

"I'm glad he's been there for you." Cross downed the rest of his drink. "Have you had a chance to talk to him about what we covered during our last session?"

"Yes, as a matter of fact, I did."

"Really? How did it go?"

"Actually it went better than I expected."

Cross's eyes widened with disbelief. "So Alex is accepting of your leaving?"

Lexa grimaced. "I wouldn't go as far as to say that."

"How receptive of the idea of your leaving was he?"

"Not very."

I mean, not at all.

Noticing that the pitcher on the table was empty, Cross got a full one from the deck's mini-fridge. He sat back down, refreshing both his and Lexa's glasses. "I can't tell you any details about the sessions I have with Alex, just as I can't tell him any details about yours." Cross picked up his glass and looked out over the water. "Let's just say that Alex has a long way to go before coming around to our way of thinking." He held up his glass. "Here's to sweet compromise."

Lexa clinked her glass against her doctor's.

Compromise? Sure, as long as I don't compromise myself. As for my twin, he'll never compromise until he—or both of us are—in the grave.

CHAPTER NINETEEN

LONELY REPAST

Bastian stood staring up at the campus's dark pyramid. Struggling against surrendering to indifference, his attention was drawn to one of Paige's memorial banners, which lay ragged and trampled beside an overflowing trash canister. Bastian shook his head in bitter defeat, pulled his flask out of his pocket, and took a long drink.

Lexa came up behind him and rested her head against his back.

He took another swig from his near empty flask and confessed, "God, I really miss the conceited bitch."

"Me too," Lexa said.

Bastian laughed. "She was so good at narcissism she made it look almost mannerly." He motioned to the pile of trash left over from the memorial service. "Isn't that ironic symbolism?"

Lexa glanced over at the mound of garbage that, just a little while ago, was extravagant décor placed in remembrance of Paige's life, and in tribute to her accomplishments on this Earth.

"We go through life struggling to always look our best," Bastian said. "Wearing nice clothes, driving cool cars, putting on expensive makeup and perfume, having perfect hair and toned physiques. Why all the bother?" He poured a mouthful of scotch down his throat. "When it's over, we all end up in a trash heap, discarded and alone."

"The only things we have that last are the things we leave behind."

Bastian scoffed. "The only thing most of us leave behind is our names carved in stone."

"No, we leave behind our memories. That is, memories of us are left behind," Lexa argued.

"Yeah, maybe for a while," Bastian conceded. "But memories fade, it's their nature. Maybe they fade so we can get on with our lives."

Some memories never fade.

Lexa moved closer and faced her inebriated friend. "I want to ask you something, and I want you to tell me the truth."

Bastian took a healthy swig and asked, "Is there a reason why I wouldn't?"

"Maybe. I don't know." Lexa moved in closer and locked eyes with Bastian. "What were you and Simms arguing about?"

Fuck me. Bastian looked down at the ground. "You saw that shit, huh?"

"Yes, I did." Lexa put her hand under Bastian's chin and raised his head back up to reconnect with her stare. "Were you arguing over something to do with Paige?"

144

"No, it was about the jobs Storm promised us." His voice sounded sincere, but his eyes were darting, his gaze settling anywhere but Lexa's stare.

"The other day at Angel's Gate, you said the text Paige got the night she died was probably from Storm," she noted.

Not knowing how to respond, Bastian fiddled with his flask.

Lexa struggled more with herself than with her unresponsive friend. *Do I really want to know?*

"Why did you say that, Bastian?"

Yes, I want to know.

"Because he was fucking her," Bastian finally revealed.

Unable to readily digest the scandalous revelation, Lexa sought solace from the age-old defense mechanism called denial. "No way. She would've told me."

Wouldn't she?

"Well, she didn't," Bastian spat. "I found out from Simms a few months ago. Paige was getting too serious and Storm wanted out."

"That's what you and Simms were arguing about?"

Bastian mouthed "Yeah" and took another swig while Lexa, disheartened and bewildered, stood questioning herself at the base of the pyramid.

Am I that socially inept? Paige and Storm? How could I have not known? Although looking back, it was so obvious.

When someone's that blind to the obvious, they've no chance catching sight of the unobvious.

"You don't think Storm and Simms had

something to do with—"

"No," Bastian said before she could even complete the sentence. "Storm may be a lecherous, self-centered bastard, but he's no psycho killer. Neither is Simms, he's harmless, the pompous little asshole."

Lexa lowered her head in ignorant confusion.

Maybe Cross was wrong. Maybe we are all just islands to ourselves. Maybe we have to be.

"How can we ever be sure we know a person?" Lexa asked. "I mean really know them?"

Without a trace of self-consciousness or embarrassment, Bastian let loose a loud, scotch-laced belch. "Beats me. I'm having a hard enough time just getting to know myself. How 'bout you?"

"How about me what?"

"You know yourself yet?"

Lexa didn't respond. She cast her eyes down to the faded concrete beneath her.

Do I know myself? No, not yet. But I feel that I will soon.

And there was nothing that frightened her more than the thought of finally coming face to face with herself.

CHAPTER TWENTY

CASSIE

Sitting in her darkened off-campus apartment, Cassie scanned her phone bill with her mobile phone's KNFB Reader. "*Balance due, one hundred twenty dollars and forty-three cents,*" it announced.

The faint glow of her laptop screen exposed her puzzled look. How could it be so high when hardly anybody ever called except for her mom?

A banging sound came through the computer's speakers. She snickered and sang, "Somebody's knockin'." She reached for her keypad to check her Roommates homepage, hesitating for a fleeting moment. Should she let them in? Shaking off her worry, she typed on her keyboard. A female computerized voice spoke her typewritten words aloud:

"Who's there?"

An instant message icon appeared upon the

screen, and a male computerized voice read:

"There's a package outside your door. You should go get it."

"What the fu…?" Cassie typed, and her computer said:

"Who is this?"

No reply from the sender.
Cassie typed again and the computer read:

"Please tell me who this is."

Still no reply.
Fear crept up on Cassie, a gut-wrenching, dread-laden fear, which those with sight would never understand.
Cassie picked up the phone and started dialing.

***

The shrill whistle from a kettle on the stovetop of apartment #106 drew the attention of the wheelchair bound tenant residing within. While wheeling his twisted body toward the kitchen, he brimmed with anticipation at the thought of his first sip of herbal tea. Just as he reached for the boiling kettle, the phone rang from the other side of the room.

Every fuckin' time.

The young disabled man wheeled himself over to

the phone and picked it up. "Hello?"

"Hi, I'm sorry to bother you. I'm your neighbor in 105," Cassie said over the phone.

"105?"

"Yes, the blind girl."

"Oh, hi. Is there something I can do for you?"

"Yes, please. I was hoping you wouldn't mind looking outside to see if there's a package by my door, and if there's anyone out there?"

"Sure, hold on a sec." The young man wheeled over to the front door, cracked it open, and peeked out. A large package was sitting in the empty hallway next to the door of apartment #105. "I don't see anyone, but there's a package in the hallway to the left of your door," he said into the phone. "Do you want me to roll out and get it for you?"

***

Cassie hesitated in the darkness. Why not let him get it? He did offer, after all. Didn't he?

Come on, Cass. You've come too far to start backsliding now.

"No, that's okay. Thank you for your help." She hung up the phone.

Building her resolve, Cassie picked up her white cane and started toward the door. She listened for a few moments, then unlocked and opened it.

She stuck her head out of her apartment door. "Hello? Hello?" She listened for a moment, then tentatively exited her apartment. A package was sitting about four feet from her door. She moved her cane along the wall until it struck the box, picked it up, and hurried back into her apartment.

She sat down in her desk chair with the package in her lap. A message immediately appeared on the screen, followed by the male computerized voice:

"Well, aren't you going to open it?"

Cassie placed the package on her desk and typed:

"Who are you? And how do you know I have a package?"

The on-screen/voice response came right away.

"To answer question number one, I'm the person who killed Kimber and Paige. And Palmer."

The pupils of Cassie's blind eyes dilated to their limit as she cried, "Oh my God!"

De profundis clamavi ad te, Domine.

As she reached out toward the phone on her desk, the reflection of the hooded figure's silhouette rose up and filled her laptop's monitor.

The on-screen/voice response continued:

"As for question number two, I'm standing right behind you."

Weeping for forgiveness of her sins, Cassie realized in that very moment she was already dead.

Domine, exaudi orationem meam.

Her fight-or-flight instinct kicked in and she reached out for her phone. The instant she picked it up, the hooded figure put a large hunting knife against her throat, and hissed in a long, sinister whisper, "Shush…"

Cassie's blood iced over. The hooded figure's free hand picked up the phone and hurled it across the room. Then the hooded figure took out a smartphone and typed on its keypad. A message displayed on the blind girl's computer monitor, read aloud through the speakers:

"We're going to play a game, one you should be good at—Blind Man's Bluff. You'll have sixty seconds to find the front door. If you win, I'll let you go. If you lose, I'll cut off your arms and legs."

Barely able to think, let alone speak, Cassie whimpered a desperate plea, "Please, please don't kill me…"

The hooded figure pressed the knife against Cassie's lips, then typed as the voice read through the speakers:

"No talking allowed, you sightless bitch. If you speak to me again, I'll bite off your tongue. If you scream for help, I'll rip off your jaw. Do you understand?"

Cassie timidly tendered her surrender.

The hooded figure knelt and removed Cassie's shoes and socks, then sheathed the knife and turned on all the lights.

Cassie sat in private darkness in her now brightly-lit apartment. Trembling uncontrollably, she listened to the hooded figure rowdily rearranging the furniture. Eventually the noise stopped, and the hooded figure walked up and stood still and silent in front of Cassie, staring into her hollow eyes.

Seconds seemed like hours as Cassie strained to hear any noise that could give her a clue as to the hooded figure's whereabouts, but no such noise was afforded. After several minutes of dread-filled silence, the sound of a zipper opening sliced across Cassie's eardrums. Several more minutes filled with mysterious sounds passed by.

Without warning the hooded figure grabbed Cassie's arms and yanked her up out of her chair, binding her wrists together with duct tape, her hands folded in front of her chest as if in prayer.

Images of Cassie's life, childhood images prior to the accident that claimed her sight, flashed behind her eyes, and then only feelings adrift in blackness from that time until this very moment.

The hooded figure took out a mini-tape recorder, leading Cassie to the center of the room. She struggled to keep her balance as the hooded figure spun her around and around. The hooded figure released the barefooted Cassie and typed on the smartphone keypad.

The voice from the computer's speakers' recited:

"Remember, sixty seconds."

The figure pressed the play button on the recorder and a synthesized voice started the countdown:

"Sixty...fifty-nine...fifty-eight..."

Cassie steadied her balance, stretched out her arms, and slowly moved forward.

"Fifty-three...fifty-two...fifty-one..."

Cassie took a few steps forward and screamed when she stepped onto a cluster of thumbtacks. When she dropped to the floor, several more tacks stuck into her hands and legs. Whimpering, Cassie inched backward and pulled out the tacks.

"Forty-two...forty-one...forty..."

She stood up and stumbled into her desk. *Why, Lord? Why me?*

"Thirty-five...thirty-four...thirty-three..."

She moved along the edge of the desk, screaming when a butcher's knife taped to one of the desk's legs sliced her hip. Sobbing, Cassie staggered back and pressed the heel of her hand upon her gushing wound.

"Twenty-seven... twenty-six... twenty-five..."

She turned one-hundred and eighty degrees and headed toward her rear, taking hold of the crucifix hanging from a chain around her neck. "The Lord is my shepherd, I shall not want. He leads me…"

"Twenty-two... twenty-one... twenty..."

Cassie cried out when she stepped on a large mousetrap. She fell forward into several more traps strewn about the floor.

Please, God, I don't want to die.

"Seventeen... sixteen... fifteen..."

She shook the traps off her hands and crawled toward her right.

Goddammit, help me!

"Twelve... eleven... ten..."

Desperate and facing the end of the fatal countdown, Cassie leaped forward with blind faith and crashed head-first into her front door.

Thank you, Lord!

She desperately scrambled for the doorknob. "Thank y—" Her prayer of thanks was interrupted by her screams of agony as she closed her hand around the razor-blade covered front doorknob.

"Seven... six... five..."

Fueled with unimaginable desperation to escape, Cassie tightened her grip on the doorknob, crying out in anguish when the razors cut deep into her hands, and desperately attempted to turn the knob.

"Two...one. Game over."

A defeated and bloodied Cassie sat weeping on the floor with her hands still grasping the razor-covered doorknob.

The hooded figure walked over to Cassie, knelt, and wrapped a long piece of duct tape about her head, covering her mouth several times. The hooded figure gripped her right bicep tightly, and with a hunting knife, carved into her arm just below the shoulder. Cassie's muffled screams echoed behind her apartment door.

***

In a filthy, fully lit room the hooded figure sat. Countless pictures of Lexa lined the walls from floor to ceiling. The monitor's skull cursor moved over Cassie's profile picture, and with a single click of the mouse, was replaced with a photograph of her blood-soaked, dismembered corpse.

CHAPTER TWENTY-ONE

FRIENDS LIST

Lexa's delicate hands spread soapy lather over her supple body, pulsating jets of water raining down from the shower nozzle like cleansing tears. White suds of shampoo streaked the dark pall draped over her head, washing down and cascading across a veneer of wet, tanned skin. Lexa had always enjoyed taking long showers, since that was the one place where she could be truly alone with herself. The calming sensation of hot jetting water helped soothe the pain seething behind her brow. She became aware of a building urge to open her eyes, and after a few moments of resistance, she did. Much to her dismay, the colorless streams of heated water started to spiral, and she lost herself once more, her essence retreating into the universe of her own mind.

FRIENDS LIST

***

Naked and still covered with soap from the shower, Lexa finds herself standing in front of her parents' burning cabin. Although the heat emanating from the flames gradually starts to ignite the soapy lather covering her nude body, even as her body begins to blister and blacken, Lexa stands still and silent, oblivious to the fire searing her flesh. After a few moments, her naked twin brother Alex enters her peripheral vision. He stands beside his sister and takes her hand. When she turns her head toward him, he smiles and points up to the sky. When Lexa looks upward, a cloudburst of rain pelts down upon her, her brother, and the cabin. The rain turns to blood, gradually dousing the fire burning Lexa and the cabin.

***

The ringing phone shut down Lexa's dark illusion and thrust her back into reality. Wrapped in a towel and still dripping wet, she hurried out of the bathroom toward her desk and picked up the phone.

"Hello?"

"Thank God. Are you okay?" Alex asked frantically.

"Yeah, I'm fine."

What the hell? Now I can't even take a shower without you trying to climb in there with me?

She sighed. "What's the matter, Alex?"

"What's the ma...when's the last time you checked your room?"

Lexa snickered and said, "I'm standing in it right now."

"No, your Roommates room."

"I don't know, a few days maybe. Where've you been all day?"

"Following a hunch. I'll fill you in later. Right now I need you to log on to your Roommates page."

"Okay, just give me a few minutes to finish my shower."

"Now goddammit!"

"Okay!" Lexa plopped down on her bed, put down the phone, opened her laptop, and logged onto the Roommates website. The Roommates homepage displayed on the monitor. A door appeared with the name plate "LEXA'S ROOM." The door opened to reveal Lexa's avatar. The avatar gave a welcoming wave and headed into the middle of the virtual room. Lexa picked her phone back up. "I'm in. Now what?"

"Look at your friends list," Alex said urgently.

Lexa moved her fingertip across the laptop's touchpad. She clicked the "BEST MATES" icon page and a new page opened full-screen on the monitor. The page listed Lexa's best friends, with their corresponding photographs, in numeric order.

"Oh my God…"

She dropped the phone. The number one spot was ominously blank with the words "PHOTO PENDING" labeled above. After being moved down a notch from number one, Kimber now held the number two spot on the list and her photo showed her decapitated head lying in her lap. Paige followed in the number three spot, with a picture of her hanging from the Queensbay Bridge. Palmer's burned remains ranked number four on the list. Cassie's dismembered corpse showed up fifth on the list. The page still showed the original photos of CK sixth, Bastian seventh, Dr. Cross eighth, Senator Storm ninth, Simms tenth...

As Lexa stared at the screen, it burst into flames. The laptop melted down into the bed as the sounds of knocking and indistinct voices grew in the background. Lexa sat in silence, large patches of flesh blistering and smoldering over her body. Boiling blood gushed from her wounds, her body caught fire and blackened. The flames spread quickly to the walls and scurried toward the ceiling. The flames engulfed the bedroom and then abruptly extinguished.

Lexa found herself physically undamaged and sitting in front of her laptop inside her unspoiled bedroom. Still half in shock from the vision, she saw her bedroom door swing open in the reflection of her laptop's monitor. Exhausted and reeling from the assaults on her psyche, she slid off the bed and landed on the floor as Captain Styles rushed in with her gun drawn.

"Are you all right?" Styles shouted while scanning the room for signs of danger.

No, I am not fucking all right. Would you be?

"I-I don't know," Lexa said.

Aunt Amanda rushed into the doorway and screamed when she saw the post-mortem pictures of Kimber, Paige, Palmer, and Cassie on the computer screen.

Styles holstered her gun. "Get dressed, you're

coming with me."

Lexa snatched her clothes off the bed, ran into the bathroom, and shut the door.

***

Lexa threw her clothes down on the vanity and stood half in shock in front of her bathroom mirror. With tears raining down her face, her mind blurred from her prescriptions, she took off the towel draped around her. Without warning, her reflection changed her eye color from sea-green to dead orange and said in a sinister tone of voice, "Lexa…time to learn who you really are."

Lexa dropped her towel to the floor and stood naked facing her mirror image.

No, she's not really there.

She closed her eyes tightly.

One…two…three…

Lexa's reflection laughed. "You think counting will make me go away? I couldn't leave if I wanted to. I'm *you*!"

With her eyes still shut, Lexa continued her count. *Five…six…*

"It's your fault, you know," said Lexa's reflection. "It's your fault they're all dead!"

Eight…nine…ten.

Lexa opened her eyes to find herself encircled by her deceased friends. Kimber's decapitated body sat on the toilet with its fried head resting in its lap; Paige's lifeless remains hung by a noose swinging from the ceiling; Palmer's incinerated carcass lay smoldering in the bathtub; and Cassie's cut up corpse lay limp in front of the bathroom door. The gruesome sight of mutilated friends sent her shrinking down to the floor.

"They'd still be alive if it wasn't for you," Lexa's mirror image taunted.

While she cowered in the middle of all this madness, time seemed to slow down and then stop altogether.

This must be insanity. What else could it be?

After realizing these visions weren't going away anytime soon, she resolved to get dressed, even if she had to do it amidst all this horror around her.

"Their blood is on your hands, Lexa!" screamed her reflection. "If you don't believe me, why don't you ask them?"

Lexa almost passed out when she looked down and saw Kimber's fried head pry open its melted lips and speak the words, "Your hands…"

Then Paige opened her eyes and looked at Lexa. "Your hands…"

Palmer, whose head is charred to the bone like the rest of his body, stretched wide its mouth and uttered, "Your hands…"

Lastly, Cassie's carved face moved what's left of its mouth and said, "Your hands…"

The words bombarded Lexa from all sides like a mental blitzkrieg, leaving her with only one retreat—to flee inward into herself, toward the ever present spiral at the center of her mind. However, as inviting as the arms of oblivion seemed at the moment, she chose not to lose herself. Not just yet. Instead, Lexa steadied herself, stepped over Cassie, and opened the door.

Her reflection and her dead friends went on shouting, "Your hands! Your hands! Your hands!"

***

Lexa emerged from the bathroom with the voices still echoing in her ears. She shut the door and stepped over to Captain Styles, who was sitting on the bed with the laptop.

"I'm ready now," Lexa said.

"Good," Styles replied. "Let's go."

CHAPTER TWENTY-TWO

INCREASED DECEASED

Styles drove through the city like all cops drove, even when off-duty—fast and aggressively, occasionally glancing at the passenger beside her. Lexa sat in near shock, her head tilted toward her window and her glazed eyes staring off into nothingness.

Without turning her head she asked Styles, "Cassie and Palmer are dead, aren't they?"

"We found Mr. Randolph's burned remains on the bottom of his parents' Jacuzzi," Styles confirmed.

Tears started to build in Lexa's expressionless eyes.

"Ms. Lovette's body was at her apartment. Totally dismembered."

Lexa covered her face and wept.

***

Captain Styles parked the unmarked police car in front of the Long Beach Police Station. Captain Styles and Lexa exited the car and hurried inside the building, going straight to the captain's office, where CK and Bastian were anxiously waiting. Styles closed the door and the three friends embraced.

After hours of by-the-book questioning, Lexa, CK, and Bastian quietly sat in patent leather chairs while Captain Styles paced.

"I want the goddamned FBI to take charge of this investigation!" Bastian screamed. "Maybe they can do something to keep the rest of us alive because *you* haven't done dick, lady."

Styles strode over to Bastian and loomed over him. "First of all, it's Captain," she retorted. "Second, I have detectives monitoring the Roommates website twenty-four/seven, specifically the homepages of your so-called Magnificent Seven."

"You mean what's left of us," Bastian snorted.

"That's how we learned about Mr. Randolph and Ms. Lovette," Styles told them.

"Is there any way to find out who changed the pictures on my friends list?" Lexa asked.

"We traced the IP address of the user who hacked your account and altered your page. It belongs to one of the hundreds of public terminals at your university's library."

"A simple no would've sufficed," Bastian muttered.

Styles pulled the reins on her short temper, and with exaggerated politeness said, "I'm sorry the wheels of justice aren't spinning faster, Mr. Shadwell. Trust me, I'm going to have every available detective working round-the-clock until we catch this killer."

"Really? Is that supposed to make us sleep better tonight?" Bastian held up his hand and dramatically extended one finger, then another, then another, and yet another. "Four of our friends are dead, Captain. They're fucking *dead*, and you have jack for a suspect and shit for a motive."

"We're doing our best, Mr. Shadwell. As far as suspects are concerned, forensics suggests that Ms. Clark, Ms. Turner, Mr. Randolph, Ms. Lovette, and Mr. Randolph's companion Ms. Denton were all murdered by the same perpetrator. As for motive, we have uncovered one lead. Except for Ms. Denton, who we feel was just at the wrong place at the wrong time..." Bastian snorted, "all of the victims were killed in the order they appeared on your friends list, Ms. Rhodes."

Lexa displayed a look of refuted culpability.

Captain Styles turned to Bastian. "And you're next on the list, Mr. Shadwell."

Bastian looked at Lexa, then back at Captain Styles. "Are you going to put me—*us*—in protective custody or something?"

"No," Styles stated.

Bastian shook his head in disbelief. "No?"

"We can't put civilians into protective custody unless they're witnesses to a crime and there's a threat of them coming into harm's way prior to their

165

testimony at trial."

Bastian exploded. "I can't fucking believe what I'm fucking hearing. How many more of us have to die before you get off your ass and *do something*?"

"We enforce the law, Mr. Shadwell. What we don't do is provide private protection." Styles looked at them one by one. "There are several security companies I can refer you to. If you can't afford to hire private security, I suggest you stay with family or friends until we capture the murderer. There is safety in numbers."

"That's it?" Bastian screeched. "That's all you have to say, that there's safety in numbers?" He shoved his chair backward and jumped up. "Well you better check your math, lady, because in less than two weeks we've gone from seven to three, and I don't..." Bastian stopped mid-sentence and shook his head in absolute frustration. "What the fuck am I doing here?" He walked over to Styles. "Here, you like numbers so much, here's one for you." Bastian flipped Captain Styles the middle finger, brushed past her, and rushed out the door muttering a string of colorful expletives.

While Styles struggled to keep her professional composure, CK patted Lexa's arm. "Come on, I'll take you home."

"Captain Styles, Dr. Cross is on my list too."

"I've already informed him of the situation, as well as Senator Storm and Terrence Simms who follow Cross on your list." Captain Styles opened the door. "I'll be in touch."

***

When Styles was heading down a crowded corridor, the appointment reminder alarm on her cell phone chimed. She took out her phone and read the message:

Doc Latham—6 P.M.

Fuck me.

She hesitated for a moment, then spun and headed back down the opposite way toward the district's psychiatrist's office.

***

Styles knocked on the door and stepped into the office of Dr. Thomas Latham.

He looked up and smiled. "Ah, Captain Styles, come in, come in."

Styles shut the door and helped herself to the chair in front of Dr. Latham's desk.

Dr. Latham clicked his mouse and opened up Styles's file on the laptop in front of him. The file onscreen read:

Intelligence quotient—high; severe trauma in early childhood; father fixation; abandonment issues; need to be admired—sees her role as protector of society, with emphasis on law and order, high focus on criminal apprehension.

"Anytime you're ready, Doc," Styles chided. "I'm in a bit of a hurry.

Dr. Latham focused his attention on the captain.

"I heard about the case you're working."

Styles shot him a contemptuous glance. "So what did you hear, Doc?"

"I heard you're hunting a vicious psychopath."

"You heard correctly."

"Interesting," Dr. Latham remarked, his voice soft. "I know how you must be feeling right now."

"You don't know shit about how I'm feeling, Doc. Look at yourself. How could you know anything about how I feel?" *You presumptuous fuck,* she thought but didn't say aloud.

Without the slightest trace of umbrage, Dr. Latham asked, "Why don't you think I can empathize with your situation, Captain Styles?"

"Because you deal with psych*es* and I deal with psych*os*. You sit here in your office sifting through peoples' emotional baggage while I'm out in the world sifting through blood and brains spilled by some fuckin' maniac." Styles adjusted herself in her seat. "People like you are hands-off and people like me get their hands dirty. Is that *why* enough for you, Doc? Now if you'll excuse me, there's a psychopath somewhere out there that deserves my attention more than you do."

Just as the captain reached the door, Latham called out, "Styles…"

Still facing the closed door in front of her, Styles said, "Yeah?"

"Answer one question."

"What?"

"The grieving family members of murder victims…when you look into their grief-stricken faces, what is it that you see?"

Styles stood for a brief moment in reflective silence, then yanked open the door and slammed it closed behind her without responding.

***

Blindsided by Latham's question, Styles took a moment to figure out which direction she should take. After a while, she leaned against the wall of the corridor.

What do I see when I look into their faces, Doc? I see myself.

***

Lexa and CK exited the police station and saw Bastian on the sidewalk lighting a cigarette, still grumbling to himself.

"Can't protect civilians indefinitely," Bastian grunted. "Thanks for nothing. Call you when I'm dead, you useless fuck!"

"Bastian, please," CK said, "just calm down."

"Calm down?" Bastian shouted. "Some psycho is using your wannabe girlfriend's friends list as a murder roster, and I'm supposed to calm down? There's not enough drugs on the planet to calm me down. Wanna know why, CK?" Bastian stabbed a finger at Lexa. "'Cause I'm next on her goddamn list." He looked directly at Lexa. "Thanks for being my friend, *sweetheart*."

Lexa turned away in a desperate attempt to conceal the guilt-ridden tears welling up in her eyes.

CK sensed the pain caused by that last spiteful remark that Lexa was trying to hide. He yanked Bastian closer and snarled, "Leave her alone! None of this is her fault!"

"Yeah? Well anyway, it's every man for himself time. If you need me I'll be at the all-night Denny's until further fucking notice."

He stalked away mumbling to himself.

"CK," Lexa said, "can we go to your place for a while?"

*Can we? You're asking me **can** we?*

"Sure." CK fought to conceal his building excitement.

Damn straight we can.

Lexa hugged him. "Thanks. It's just that I can't face Aunt Amanda and Uncle Claude. Not right now."

CHAPTER TWENTY-THREE

DO YOU FEEL LIKE I DO

CK and Lexa stepped into his apartment, a modest, garden variety, off-campus student housing unit.

"Please excuse the mess," he said, and flipped on the lights.

Lexa walked over to the couch, stopping in front of it when she saw it was covered with clothes. CK hurried over and collected most of his clothes off the couch.

"Have a seat." Lexa sat down. "Can I get you something?" asked CK.

You name it. All you have to do is ask.

"Some water?"

"Comin' up." CK practically leaped into the kitchen. "I'm making coffee. You want some?"

"No, thanks." Lexa glanced around the messy apartment. After a casual once-over, her attention

171

was strangely drawn to a dim light flickering in the space between the bottom of the bedroom door and the floor.

When he finished fumbling around in the kitchen, CK returned holding a glass of water. "Here you go." When Lexa reached for the glass, their fingers brushed against each other's. They both blushed and turned away. CK stood awkwardly in front of her for a couple of seconds before sitting down on the couch next to her.

Lexa took three capsules out of her purse and swallowed them with a gulp of water. She rubbed her forehead and confessed, "These headaches are driving me insane."

"Sorry," CK said lamely. "Ever try acupressure?"

"No."

"I took a couple of instructional seminars last semester.

Yeah right. I learned it from my mom.

"You can block pain by putting pressure on the right spot." CK paused in anticipation. "Do you want to try it?"

"At this point I'm willing to try anything."

Yes!

CK took Lexa's glass and placed it on the coffee table. "Okay, lie back against me and let me know when the pain stops." Lexa bashfully leaned back against CK's chest.

CK gently applied pressure to different spots on Lexa's head. "There. Right there," she said. "The pain's stopping."

CK focused his massage in that spot.

Should I...or shouldn't I?

He cleared his throat and said, "You really mean a lot to me, Lexa."

"You mean a lot to me too, CK."

CK softly chuckled and continued massaging.

Go ahead, this might be your last chance.

"I can't believe I'm considering telling you this..."

"Telling me what?"

"How I really feel. That I want to be more than just your friend."

"CK..."

"Let me finish. I don't know if I'll ever have the guts to say this again." He took a deep breath. "When I'm with you, it hurts not being able to tell you how much I love you. I'm sorry to drop this on you now, but I've seen how short life can be, and I don't want to die without letting you know how much I want you."

Lexa sat up and faced CK, who let out a big sigh of relief. "Whoa! I really needed to let that out. But no worries, I won't let this ruin our—"

Lexa kissed CK passionately on the lips. "I want you too, CK," she said when she pulled away. "I have for a long time. I just didn't know how to tell you."

Fuck me.

"So where do we go from here?"

"You're the one in the driver's seat, Mr. Kane."

CK caressed Lexa's face.

No more wasted time.

He kissed her with desperate passion. As his hand moved up her inner thigh, Lexa stopped and pulled away.

CK sat back in disappointment. "I'm sorry, I didn't mean to—"

"No, it's not you, it's me," Lexa said.

Go ahead, tell him so he'll understand.

"I've...I've never been with a man before." She sat up and wrapped her arms around her legs. "I know it sounds stupid, but I've been saving myself for my wedding night."

CK reached over and caressed her cheek. "I don't think it's stupid. Some things are well worth the wait."

Lexa smirked. "But you're right, about how short life can be. All my life I haven't done much living." She moved closer to CK. "I think I'll start now." As she placed her lips on his, the smoke alarm blared.

CK gritted his teeth. "Dammit, not now."

"What is that?"

"The smoke alarm. The damned thing's hypersensitive." He gave Lexa a quick peck on the lips. "Don't move, I'll be right back." He hopped off the couch and raced into the kitchen.

"The damned thing goes off all the time!" he yelled. The light flickering underneath CK's bedroom door caught Lexa's attention again. Still in the kitchen, CK barked out, "It's stupid having a smoke alarm in the kitchen anyway."

Lexa stood and headed toward the bedroom door. The smoke alarm went off when she reached the door. Lexa put her ear to the door.

Don't do it. You may not like what you find in there.

She opened the bedroom door and saw CK's desktop computer. A screensaver picture rotation of the Mag Seven was displayed on the monitor.

Shit!

The unexpected ring of her phone almost made Lexa jump out of her skin. She ran over to the coffee table and dug her phone out of her purse. "Hello?"

"Where the fuck are you?" Alex screamed through the phone's earpiece.

"Alex! I'm glad it's you. Cassie and Palmer are dead."

"I know, Cross told me." Alex held the phone to his ear with his shoulder as he typed on Lexa's laptop. *"But where are you?"*

"Styles picked me up and took me to the police station, then CK brought me here to his apartment."

"You're where? Listen to me, Sis, I need you to get out of there right now. Don't ask me why and don't say anything to CK. Just get outside and run and don't stop running."

"Alex, what the hell are you—"

"Shut up and listen. There's two reasons why you shouldn't be there. One, CK's on your friends list, so the killer could be in his apartment right now waiting to kill him."

Lexa anxiously looked around the apartment.

"And two, CK could be the killer."

"What?"

"He has a weird, obsessive crush on you. Everyone knows it except you."

"He just told me. But he's not weird or anything, he's just shy."

"Lexa, I'm telling you, he acts like he wants you all to himself. And sometimes he gives your friends this creepy stare, like they're standing in his way or something."

"You're fishing in a shallow pond, X-Man." Lexa walked back toward CK's bedroom. "Besides, I'm not a woman that men go crazy psycho over."

"You are. At least to him you are. And with the others dead, he has four less obstacles between you and him." Lexa glanced into the bedroom at the computer monitor. A hideous picture flashed on the screen, then changed to a picture of CK. *"Only Bastian stands between him and the number one spot as your Best Mate."*

"Hold on a sec." Lexa stepped into the bedroom and over to the desk. Her eyes widened in horror when she saw a picture of Kimber's severed head held over a pot of boiling oil displayed on the computer's monitor. The picture dissolved to Paige lying unconscious atop the Queensbay Bridge, and then to Palmer ablaze in the Jacuzzi. Finally Palmer's picture changed to one of Cassie's dismembered torso.

While Lexa had been standing in front of the computer monitor, a dark silhouette slowly approached her from behind. Just as the images on the monitor were about to send her over the edge, she felt the sensation of warm breath against her neck. "What are you doing?" CK whispered into her ear.

Lexa spun around and stumbled backward yelling, "It was you! You killed them!"

CK moved toward Lexa. "What are you talking

about?" Then the gruesome display on the monitor caught his eye. "What the hell…?" After viewing a complete rotation of pictures, he turned toward Lexa with a face swathed with genuine confusion.

"Stay away from me," she warned, trying to increase the distance between them.

"Lexa, please, I swear I don't know how those got on there."

Lexa remembered then she was holding her phone. She put it up to her ear and cried, "Alex, help me! I'm trapped!"

"Listen, I don't know what's going on, but we're friends, right?" CK moved slowly toward Lexa. "I'd never do anything to hurt you."

Lexa backed away and shrank down into a corner as CK drew ever closer.

"There's nothing to be afraid of." CK held out his hand toward Lexa. "Trust me."

Lexa held her hand out toward CK's, then kicked him square in the groin. When he doubled over in pain, she delivered an uppercut that sent him to the floor.

Lexa jumped to her feet, leapt over CK, and raced for the front door.

She burst through the door and ran screaming from the apartment. CK stumbled out the door and chased after her, screaming, "Lexa! Lexa, wait!"

Lexa ran out to the street. With her flight mode now in overdrive, she turned her head and saw CK following close behind.

CK screamed, "Lexa, look out!"

Lexa whipped around and collapsed as a campus patrol car screeched to a halt mere inches in front of her.

Two security officers leaped out and hurried toward Lexa.

"Help me, please!" She pointed at CK. "He killed my friends and now he's trying to kill me!"

One officer covered Lexa while the other drew his weapon and pointed it at CK. "You!" he shouted. "Don't move!"

CK put up his hands. "Wait a minute!"

"He has pictures of our dead friends on his computer," Lexa sobbed.

The officer tried to steady his shaky aim on CK and ordered, "On the ground—now!" CK acted like he was complying, then took off running. The officer fired several shots, all of which missed their target. He holstered his weapon and chased after CK, only to lose him shortly afterward in the dark.

While the other officer got on the radio, Lexa cowered in front of the patrol car and wept.

Is Alex right? Am I really the cause of all of this? Am I the reason my friends are dead?

***

Amanda, Claude, and Alex stood worriedly on the porch as a police car pulled in front of the house. Lexa jumped out of the car and ran into the arms of her family.

"We almost lost you tonight," Amanda sobbed.

Lexa nodded tearfully. "You would have if it wasn't for Alex."

Claude walked over to talk to the police officer.

A car screeched to a halt behind the patrol car.

Bastian hopped out of the car, running up to embrace Lexa. "Alex called me. What the hell happened?"

Claude rejoined the others and the police car drove away.

Lexa took Bastian's arm. "Could we please go somewhere?"

Bastian's eyes silently sought permission from Claude, who motioned his approval with a prolonged wink. "Sure. I know somewhere quiet and safe we can go."

Amanda stepped toward her niece. "Lexa, I don't think you should—"

"Let her go," Claude said, taking his wife by the arm and pulling her back. "She'll be all right." He set his eyes upon Bastian and, by facial expression alone, bade him, *"You better watch over my niece."* After giving Claude a nod of assurance, Bastian walked Lexa to his car, got her inside, and drove away.

CHAPTER TWENTY-FOUR

UNDER THE BRIDGE

Lexa and Bastian were sitting on a bench underneath the St. Vincent Thomas Bridge.

"It doesn't make any fuckin' sense." Bastian handed Lexa his flask.

"I know, it doesn't." She took a sip from the flask, handing it back to Bastian.

"You know, it's kinda funny."

"What is?"

"The lengths we sometimes have to go through to learn something. Ever read *Catch-22*?"

Lexa nodded. "Yeah."

I've done more than read it. I live it.

"Well I didn't, I saw the movie. Never really understood the idea of a no-win situation until now. If CK isn't the killer, then I'm fucked cause the real killer's still out there and I'm next on the list." Bastian took a healthy swig from his flask. "And if

CK *is* the killer, then I'm fucked 'cause he's on the loose and I'm next on the list. So either way, I'm fucked. Catch-22." Bastian emptied his flask down his throat. "After I take you home, I'm gonna dig a deep hole to hide in."

"Can you dig one that fits both of us?"

Bastian snickered and put his arm around Lexa. After a quiet minute or so, he mustered enough drunken courage to put forth a question he'd been hesitant to ask. "Not meaning to pile more shit on you tonight, but how come we never got together?"

Under dried tears, Lexa smiled bashfully. "I dunno."

"What, I wasn't your type?"

Lexa giggled. "No. It's just that you're…"

"An asshole?"

"At times. Yeah, kinda."

Bastian nodded. "I can see that." They both grinned. "At least you're honest."

"I try to be."

That is, with everyone but myself.

Bastian pocketed the empty flask, pulled out a full one, twisted off the cap, and took a drink.

"I know I talk a lotta shit," Bastian continued. "I do…but I do it because if I don't, I'm scared no one would hear me. Sounds stupid, huh?"

Bastian's words gave Lexa newfound vision that, for the first time since meeting, allowed her to see through her friend's coat of armor—an armor forged from a mixture of cynicism and derision.

"No, it doesn't." She gave him a friendly peck on the cheek. Feeling a sudden wave of anxiety, Lexa reached into her purse and took out a couple of pills from one of her medicine bottles. She pointed to Bastian's flask. "Mind if I see that for a minute?"

Bastian handed it to her. "Sure it's okay to drink that with those pills?"

"Do you really think it makes any difference? After all that's happened and all that's still to come?"

"Guess I see your point."

"Damn straight." She popped the pills into her mouth and downed them with a mouthful of scotch. Grimacing, she handed the flask back to Bastian. "You know, no matter who you are, no matter what you do, no matter how hard you try, or how much you love, life still gives us pain. An abundance of it."

"True, life can suck, and often times it does, but in the end, it's all we've got." Bastian shook his flask. "Sorry, I tend to get philosophical when I'm drunk. Think you're special? That you were given more to suffer than anyone else?" Bastian shook his head. "Life's a deck of cards and we're all dealt a shitty hand in some form or another. But like my dad used to say, a man's gotta do what a man's gotta do, and when he doesn't, a woman does it'."

Lexa laughed. "Your dad sounds like a funny guy."

"Yeah, he was. He died when I was little."

The image of her parents' burning cabin flashed in Lexa's head and two tears run down her cheek. "I'm sorry," she said.

"Yeah, me too." Bastian took another swig.

A few pain-filled moments passed.

No more island. Share your pain with him.

"When I was eight, I lost both my mom and my dad."

"Wow, sorry."

"Yeah, me too." Lexa shut her eyes and desperately tried to stop the spiral her mind was being drawn toward. After an exhausting effort, the spiral stopped. Lexa opened her eyes. "So what is it that we gotta do?"

"The only thing we can do—play the hand we're dealt. As simple and corny as it sounds, it's true. It's all we can do." A flippant grin stretched over his face. "Unless you're rich enough to stack the deck like Palm—" He turned his head to hide the rush of tears, unscrewed the lid of his flask, and took an entire mouthful of scotch. Lexa scooted closer and rested her head on his shoulder. Bastian tightened the flask's lid and put his arm around her.

With only hopeless despair to use for their blanket, they sat with each other in the dark moonlight. Drinking in the shrouding darkness, Lexa said softly, "C'mon, let's go."

Bastian wrinkled his brow. "Go where?"

"To dig that hole of yours."

***

While Lexa and Bastian shared an uneasy laugh, nearby a mind was seething with murderous designs; the mind of the hooded figure who was watching them from atop the illuminated bridge.

CHAPTER TWENTY-FIVE

ON OUR OWN

Several hours after leaving with Bastian, Lexa finally arrived home to find Alex anxiously awaiting her near the fireplace while Aunt Amanda and Uncle Claude held vigil on the couch. After wiping her shoes on the doormat, she stepped into the entryway and closed the door.

"Where have you been?" Amanda asked shakily. "You were gone for so long I thought…"

Lexa ignored her aunt and made a beeline toward her twin brother. They embraced for the longest time, then sat in front of the roaring fireplace whispering to each other.

Hurt by, but understanding of, their niece's snub, Aunt Amanda and Uncle Claude decided to give them their privacy.

With flames as their backdrop, Lexa and Alex communicated in a way that was beyond the understanding of their aunt and uncle. It was as if they were preborn babes clasped together in their mother's womb, sharing feelings and thoughts by means known only to twins. When the enigmatic conversation concluded, they took their places at the chessboard. Time seemed to move in slow motion as the twins stared down in silence at the playing field in front of them, both deeply and totally immersed in strategic thought. Sitting unobtrusively on the couch, Claude read his newspaper while Amanda crocheted next to him. Every once in a while they snuck a peek over toward the chess game taking place next to the fireplace.

Lexa moved a chess piece.

Lexa: You saved my life.

Alex moved a chess piece. *I love you more than you'll ever know. You are my life.*

Lexa moved another piece. *How could I ever leave you?*

Lexa: You've always been there for me.

Alex: And I always will be.

Alex moved a chess piece and grinned. *Check, and mate.*

Lexa examined the chessboard, grinning back at Alex.

Lexa: You win.

Alex: Was there ever any doubt? You gonna pay up and make the call?

Lexa nodded.

Alex motioned toward the stairs. *Shall we?*

Claude and Amanda watched worriedly as the game finally ended. Amanda started to speak, but her husband cut her off with a gentle tug on her arm. Lexa and Alex got up from the chess table and headed up the staircase, hand in hand.

***

Lying on Lexa's bed beside her, Alex eagerly watches her pick up the phone and dial.

Dr. Cross's voice answers through the earpiece, *"Hello?"*

"Dr. Cross?"

"Lexa, is that you?"

"Yes, it's me."

"Well hi. What can I do for you?"

Lexa looks at Alex and hesitates. *Can I do this?*

Sensing that something was wrong, Dr. Cross asks, *"Lexa, what is going on with you tonight?"*

"To be honest, I've talked it over with Alex and he agrees. Your therapy isn't working and your prescriptions aren't helping, so…"

"Go on, finish it!" Alex hisses.

Lexa takes a deep breath. *I can do this.* "…so we decided I won't be using your services any longer."

"Lexa, I think we should discuss—"

"Goodbye, Dr. Cross, and don't worry, Alex is going to help me find another form of treatment." Lexa hangs up the phone and smiles at Alex.

Alex smiles back. "It's like I told you, sis, we are indivisible, and that indivisibility makes us invincible."

***

The telephone rang. Claude ruffled his newspaper while Amanda set aside her crochet hooks and answered the phone. "Hello?"

"Mrs. Rhodes, this is Dr. Cross. Please forgive the lateness of the hour, but this can't wait."

Amanda held the phone away from her ear and caught Claude's attention. "What is it, doctor?" Claude moved close to his wife and listened to the receiver.

"There's something we have to discuss about Lexa. And Alex."

***

While Alex and Lexa sat talking on the bed, a knock came at the door.

"Come on in," Lexa called.

"Yeah, don't worry, we're both decent," Alex added.

Ripe with trepidation, Claude and Amanda stepped into Lexa's room and stood with their deep-seated concerns spilling forth from beneath their cheerful facades.

Gripping the doorknob for support, Amanda said, "Um, there's something we need to talk about." She pushed the door closed.

How are we going to handle this, dear Lord? How are we going to do this without Dr. Cross?

She turned to Claude with the desperation of an injured tag-team wrestler waiting to tap-out to his partner.

Catching his wife's silent plea, Claude took over. "We just got a phone call from Dr. Cross."

"That figures," Alex whispered.

"He told us..." Claude swallowed. "He told us, Lexa, that you have decided not to see him anymore. Is that true?"

"Yes, it's true," Lexa confirmed.

Amanda jumped in and asked, "Why on earth would you want to go and do that? Especially now, after all that's happened?"

"You know the sense of loss people feel when they lose a loved one?" Lexa pointed to the pit of her stomach. "The desolate void that empties the space inside where your soul should be? That's how I feel all the time."

Amanda's welling tears started to trickle down her face.

"Every single day, for as far back as I can remember, I've lived with that hollow, pain-ridden feeling," Lexa told them. "An agony of emptiness that feels like your insides have been cored out of you."

"I understand, sweetie," Claude said. "You've suffered so much at such a young age. You were so young when your parents we're killed in that fire."

Lexa shook her head. "No, Uncle Claude, you don't understand. It's not the loss of my parents that haunts me, it's the loss of myself I've had to endure."

Claude and Amanda exchanged looks of confusion. Sensing she may be sharing too much too soon, Lexa changed gears. "I want to apologize to you both for how I've been acting lately."

Claude smiled empathetically at his niece. "Your behavior was understandable, sweetheart. You've been through hell these past couple of weeks."

"Even so, there's no excuse for the way I've been treating you and Aunt Amanda." Lexa got up to hug them both. "I'm sorry, Aunt Amanda."

"I'm sorry too, my angel," Amanda blubbered from underneath a truckload of cakey foundation.

Lexa hugged her uncle next. "I'm sorry, Uncle Claude."

"I'm sorry too, sweetheart."

"Well you both should be glad to know that, with the help of a certain twin brother of mine, I've managed to piece my life together and recognize things for what they really are."

Claude and Amanda exchanged wary glances, steadying themselves for what was next to come out of the mouth of their niece.

"I finally realize that I wasn't upset with the two of you. You both were only doing what you were told would help me. The person I was really mad at was myself. I kept blaming myself for not getting better. But what I've come to learn is that my condition isn't my fault, not in any way, shape, or form." Lexa turned toward her brother. "It was Alex that finally got me to realize that."

Claude and Amanda exchanged a glance, then shot their eyes back to Lexa.

"The problem that was haunting my soul was that I couldn't stand the thought of staying here anymore and Alex couldn't stand the thought of me ever leaving. The situation was like a Gordian knot and our hands were raw from years of struggling in vain to untie it. And then the answer came to us. Well actually, it came to Alex." Her twin waggled his eyebrows several times in quick succession. "The answer was so simple. It was right there in front of us all this time. I guess it was too close for us to see."

"So what is this answer you're talking about?" Claude asked, about to lose what was left of his patience.

Lexa donned an air of triumph. "The answer is this: Alex will come with me when I leave."

"You mean you're just going to run off somewhere with Alex?" Amanda asked.

"What about your prescriptions?" asked Claude. "You've been on them for most of your life. What do you think will happen if you stop taking them cold turkey?"

"Yes, I have been on them most of my life, and I haven't gotten well yet. After years and years of taking them, I haven't gotten any better. As a matter of fact, lately I've been getting worse, even after Dr. Cross increased my dosage." Lexa reached over and took her brother by the hand. "Alex and I want to try something new. Something different that follows my new philosophy."

Claude put forth the question, "And what is this new philosophy of yours?"

"To stop looking back, like Cross always had me do, and start looking forward, to my future."

"I…we don't have a problem with this new philosophy of yours. It's other things that we have questions about."

"Other things?" Lexa asked. "What other things?"

"Like how will you survive out there, Lexa?

You've never, ever lived on your own."

"Yes, I know, but it's time I learn. Besides, I'll have Alex there with me." Lexa looked confidently at her twin. "As long as we're together, no one can stop us."

"You still have yet to answer my question, Lexa."

"What question are you referring to?"

"The question of how will you survive out there in the world."

"There's nothing to worry about. Alex and I have it all planned out."

"It doesn't sound like that to me," Claude responded. "It doesn't sound like there's any plan beyond your leaving this house. I mean seriously, how are you going to go about filling life's basic needs? Food, clothes, shelter, money…"

"I'm going to be working with Spencer Storm as a member of his staff."

Claude scoffed. "Are you telling me this future of yours is banked on a job you don't even have yet?"

"That job is as good as mine. Senator Storm said it will be there waiting for me."

Claude ran a hand through his hair in frustration. "I think you're being childish."

"So you think my dream is childish, huh?"

"No, not your dream. It's the way you intend on realizing your dream that is childish, very much so."

Amanda walked up behind her husband. "Now sweetie, you heard what your uncle said. We don't think your dreams are childish. But maybe, just *maybe*, they're a little bit out of your reach right now."

"Oh, is that what you think, puddin'?"

Amanda was knocked a little off balance by Lexa's mockery. After a few seconds, she gathered herself and went on. "I love you with all of my heart. I have from the first moment you came to live with us all those years ago. Do you know that I pray every night that you find health and happiness, my darling Lexa?"

"You say prayers for me every night?"

Isn't that something. Well, Auntie, if you've been praying for me all this time and still nothing's happened, I'd say it was time to find another prayer to pray because your prayers aren't working. If something doesn't work, you get rid of it.

"Yes, sweetie. And I think you should start praying too, Lexa." Her niece gave her a cockeyed look. "Then maybe God will cure you of all your problems."

"Really, Aunt Amanda? It's really that easy?"

"Oh shit," Alex muttered under his breath. "Here we go again."

"Yes, I do. In fact, that might be what God's waiting for, for you to pray to Him before He will heal you."

"So…all I have to do is pray, and your Lord will deliver healing unto me?"

"He's the Lord of all of us, Lexa," Amanda explained with the patience of the faithful. "And yes, He will."

"Cool. Does the Lord deliver these healings in thirty minutes or less or the healing's free, like pizza?"

Amanda's heart sank. "Lexa, how dare you disrespect the Lord!"

"Why shouldn't I?" Lexa pressed. "After all, your Lord's disrespected me my whole goddamned life."

Frustrated beyond belief, Amanda shrieked, "Why do you keep saying your Lord?"

What can I say to hurt auntie the most? Lexa cracked a wicked grin. "Because maybe I worship someone else as God."

The dire need to save her niece outweighing the shock of what she'd just heard provided Amanda the fortitude to persevere. "Lexa Rhodes!" she screamed. "Those words you spoke, whether true or not, could damn your soul to Hell!"

"Don't you two get it? I'm already there. That is, I was until Alex pulled me out."

In an attempt to defuse the bomb preparing to explode in their midst, Claude started off calm and soft-spoken. "Lexa, you know and I know that this isn't you, just like that wasn't you the other day. Now I want you to tell me who it is that put you up to this behavior. Was it Alex? It's okay, you can tell us."

Lexa and Alex shared the same look of resentment for their uncle's question. "Do you really want to know, Uncle?"

"Yes, Lexa," Claude responded. "Yes, I do."

"Okay, Uncle Claude, I'll tell you, right after you tell me why you both are so dead set against me leaving and having a life like everyone else?" Lexa got up into Claude's face. "Tell me the truth for once in your miserable fuckin' life!"

With that, Claude's patience and understanding abandoned him, and the floodgates that for years and years had been holding back untold truths sprung wide open. "Because you'll never be like everyone else, Lexa!" he yelled. "You're too messed up in the head to ever be!"

Amanda, stunned and beside herself, wailed, "Please, Claude! No…"

Claude took a brief moment to calm himself. Then in a lower voice said to his stunned niece, "I'm sorry, sweetheart. It's not your fault, it never has been. But you demanded the truth, so here it is. You never have been like everyone else, and you never will be." Alex sat like a volcano building pressure as his sister's world crumbled around her. "Look, sweetheart, you may think you're okay now," Claude said kindly, "but there's years of stuff you don't seem to remember. Stuff that'll prevent you from ever being normal, stuff that could have forced you to grow up in an institution. And if it wasn't for Dr. Cross, you probably would have." Claude glanced at his wife.

*Cross? If it wasn't for **us**, she would have.*

"And all this stuff, most of it anyway, involves the deaths of your parents. Some of the…the trouble did start before their deaths, but that centered around Alex." Claude sighed deeply. "Dr. Cross wishes to have one last session and your aunt and I agree."

Without any warning, the bitter shock of hearing her husband say what he'd said to their niece caused Amanda to collapse in a heap upon the bedroom floor.

"Amanda!" Claude stood helplessly over his wife as she lay on the floor shaking and speaking in tongues.

With her armor destroyed by the onslaught of Claude's brutally honest words, Lexa fell weeping upon her bed in utter defeat. Alex's psyche erupted with orange molten hot lava as he watched tears pour down his twin sister's face. He jumped up off the bed, and with a voice deepened by his fury, yelled into his uncle's face, "You've gone too far, asshole. Now both of you old fucks have to deal with me!"

CHAPTER TWENTY-SIX

HIDE AND SEEK

The darkened streets of the quiet neighborhoods surrounding the campus were being kept awake by sirens howling between spinning red and blue lights. Captain Styles had patrol units sweeping the last known whereabouts of her newly established main suspect.

Hidden inside a stench-filled, maggot breeding trash dumpster behind a fast food restaurant, CK peeked out from space under the dumpster's lid. Sitting amidst the rotten garbage he tried to sort through the myriad of questions bouncing around inside his brain.

What the fuck happened? What the hell was Lexa talking about? And what was that shit on my computer?

The grim reality of his situation forced CK to start questioning himself.

FRIENDS LIST

I couldn't have done anything like that to my friends, could I? How could I possibly murder my best friends and not remember? Have I gone insane and haven't realized it yet? Are the insane capable of knowing they're insane?

Realizing he wouldn't discover the answers to those questions anytime soon, he tried to figure out his next move.

What am I gonna do? What are my options? Should I just call Styles and turn myself in?

His thoughts turned from self-preservation to selfless protection.

What about Lexa? The real killer might go after her next. Who's gonna watch over her if everyone's out looking for me?

***

Captain Styles sat restlessly behind her desk coordinating the manhunt for CK. Atop her desk were two landlines, a laptop computer, two cell phones, and three police radios, one laying on the desk and two sitting on chargers. One of the landlines had been ringing for over a couple of minutes.

"Styles," she answered curtly. After listening a moment she said, "I don't give a damn about any double-shift horseshit. I need every available badge out there combing those fucking streets for that maniac, and that includes you too, Sanchez. You just stay out there and keep your eyes open, and if I catch your fat ass back here any time before dawn, I'll cook it up and serve it to you for breakfast!" She slammed down the receiver.

Lieutenant Sternn, a portly man in his mid-forties, approached Styles's desk with a steaming hot cup of coffee in his hand. "Here you go, Cap," he said, handing her the cup.

"Thanks." Styles accepted the cup and took a big drink. She set down the cup and picked up the picture of CK she had enlarged from his university identification card, held it up close in front of her face, and examined his eyes. After a long moment, she motioned to Sternn. "What do you see in these eyes? Do you see the soul of a bloodthirsty maniac?"

After a quick inspection, Sternn said, "Nope, not even close. What do you see, Cap?"

Styles studied the photo once again. "I dunno, the jury's still out on that one."

***

CK was jolted awake by a large rat climbing up his leg.

"Son-of-a-bitch!" he yelled, brushing it off in hysterical girlish fashion. He hunkered down into a corner for a few minutes to compose himself. The brazen rodent started to lure his attention.

"So, what are you up to?" CK asked aloud. The rat stared at him for a time. When sensing it was safe, it moved closer, sat up on its haunches, and sniffed toward CK's crouched legs.

What? Something down there you want?

CK shifted his legs and saw a half-rotten hamburger patty wedged between two moldy buns.

"Is this what you're after?" Like it understood CK's question, the rat stretched upward and rubbed its front paws together. "Here, dinner's on me tonight." He tossed the patty in front of the eagerly awaiting vermin. The rodent grabbed the hamburger patty with its mouth and dragged it toward the other side of the stench-filled dumpster, where a smaller female rat was patiently waiting. The sight made CK laugh. "Looks like your date turned out a lot better than mine did."

He chuckled, took a long, calming breath, and closed his eyes.

***

Captain Styles sat in the passenger's seat of an unmarked unit while Lieutenant Sternn piloted the driver's seat.

"I was wondering how long it would take before you'd go stir-crazy and hit the streets," Sternn cracked.

"Running around out there somewhere is a vicious psychopath named Kane with a penchant for choosing his victims from his wannabe girlfriend's friends list."

Confusion squatted upon Sternn's face. "A pen what?"

"A penchant. Like having a hard-on for."

"Oh, gotcha, Cap. So, what's up with Kane? What's the point of killing all of his friend's other friends?"

"I don't know for sure—yet."

"Maybe he's pissed off at her for some reason

and made up his mind that she doesn't deserve to have any friends. What do you think, Cap?"

"Maybe," Styles said. *Or he could be doing it so he can have her all to himself and be her only friend.*

***

CK opened his eyes and found himself wearing a dark and wrinkled groom's tuxedo. He was standing before a dirty altar in an oddly decorated church. The strange décor was wedding themed, but instead of having a joyous feel to it, it had a mournful one. Next to him stood his best man, Bastian, who was holding a large pewter flask in his hand. "Wanna snort?"

"No, thanks," CK whispered.

"Maybe not now, but you will soon." Bastian unscrewed the cap and started chugging down the entire contents of the flask.

CK eyed the other members of the Magnificent Seven smiling up at him from the front pew on the groom's side of the church. He smiled back at them, then tilted his head toward his best man. "Bastian?"

After letting out a muffled belch, Bastian answered, "Yeah?"

"How the hell did I get here, and what the hell's going on?"

Bastian finished off the flask and stowed it into his back pocket. "What do ya think's going on, you moron? You're marrying Lexa."

When CK's brain finished processing Bastian's words, a wide grin stretched across his face.

Is this real? Is this my dream coming true?

Even though everything unfolding around him was in contradiction with what he knew as reality, CK chose to go for broke.

"You better get back on the clock, Mr. Kane," Bastian advised the groom as the organist started playing a dark and disturbing wedding march. "Because here comes the bride."

Lexa...

CK turned to see the love of his life walking up the aisle toward him. She was wearing a dingy, off-white wedding dress, with a train that was dragging over rotten rose petals being tossed in front of her by a pair of gothic flower girls. Between black-nailed fingers, she held a bouquet of withered, long-stemmed roses, and a grayish veil hid her face. CK's initial feeling of warm elation gradually gave way to one of nauseated fear as his bride-to-be drew closer and closer. He looked at Bastian, who winked, made a hole with his left forefinger and thumb, and rapidly slid his right forefinger in and out of that hole.

"Congrats, CK," Kimber called out from the front pew. CK whirled around in time to see her head tilt down, then fall into her lap and start to sizzle, as if it was inside a deep fryer. Sitting next to Kimber was Paige, who winked at the groom just before a noose around her neck yanked her upward, suspending her twitching body over the pew. When Lexa reached the steps leading up to the altar, Palmer snapped CK a lazy salute and burst into flames, burning beyond recognition.

As the object of his affection drew dangerously

close, CK's eyes fell upon Cassie blindly waving to him as an unseen blade sliced her flesh and bone like a butcher cutting meat. All the horrid pictures of his dead friends, the ones he saw on his computer, were now materializing in the pew in front of him.

What the hell is happening to me?

As CK stood trembling in abject terror from the sights he had seen, Lexa walked up and joined him in front of the altar. He was unable to make out her face from behind the veil.

"Lexa," he gasped. "My God, what is happening?"

"Your God?" Lexa asked from behind her soiled veil. "Your God has nothing to do with any of this, my love."

"Lexa," CK begged, "please tell me what is going on!"

"Now," said Lexa, "let me show you *my* god." She raised her arm and pointed in front of them. CK slowly turned toward the altar and cast his frightened eyes upon a tall, hooded priest standing in front of them with a large, blood-stained bible in his gloved hands. The priest motioned to Lexa, who respectfully bowed her head to him. He turned his hooded head to CK, motioned once more, and opened the bible to reveal a large, bloody hunting knife concealed within the book's hollowed-out pages. The hooded priest took out the knife and held it upward with the utmost reverence.

As CK struggled desperately to hold onto what little reason he had left, Lexa asked, "Are you ready, my darling? Are you ready to lay your eyes upon your blushing bride-to-be?"

Through eyes reddened and blurred with tears, he attempted to bring into focus her veil-covered face. With shaking hands, CK reached over to lift up Lexa's veil. The moment his fingers came into contact with the fabric, she dropped her bouquet of dead flowers to the floor and CK snatched his hands away. At that moment, the hooded priest lowered the knife down to his chest, thrusting it forward into the space between the bride and groom. The hooded priest then cast his faceless gaze between Lexa and CK, as if he was offering the knife first to one and then to the other.

"No," CK told the hooded priest. "My choice is no." He reached for Lexa's hand. "C'mon, let's get the hell outta here."

The hooded priest locked his gaze on Lexa, who stared down at the bloodstained blade. From behind her filth-covered veil, she warily moved her hand toward the deadly instrument.

"No, Lexa," CK implored his bride-to-be. "I chose not to. You can too."

Lexa ran her fingers along the razor-edge of the knife, lifted up her veil, and exposed her beautiful, tear-drenched face. "Some things are chosen for us," she said. After the priest handed Lexa the knife, he reached up to pull back his hood.

***

CK startled awake inside the garbage dumpster, glancing around wildly in the darkness until the rotten stench reminded him where he was. After a few moments, he settled himself down and found a maggot-free place to squat down once again. His tired eyes scoured the dumpster until they spotted the rat and his mate, who had finished their meal and were trying to find a place to bed down for what was left of the night.

"Well, that settles it, dude," CK said amiably to the rat. "I must be going insane. Or maybe I've already arrived, but don't know it just yet."

CHAPTER TWENTY-SEVEN

A CHANGING OF MINDS

The next morning, the doorbell rang. Lexa opened it to see Dr. Cross standing on the porch.

"Hello, Lexa. I hope Claude and Amanda didn't have too much trouble last night getting you to agree to this last session."

Lexa snickered. "I wasn't the one they had trouble with."

Alex stepped out of Lexa's room and watched from the top of the staircase.

Dr. Cross looked past Lexa. "Don't they want to say goodbye?"

"They did, but Alex said they changed their minds." Lexa called up to Alex. "Let's go, X-Man." She brushed past Dr. Cross.

"You and your brother wait for me in my car," Dr. Cross instructed, heading into the living room. "I'll be there in a minute."

ROB WATSON

***

CK ran up and crouched down behind a car parked across the street from the Rhodes' house. He waited a few moments, carefully scanning the area. After a couple of deep breaths, he hurried across the street toward the house. He crept up to one of the front windows and saw the backs of the heads of two people sitting on the loveseat.

Okay, first I have to convince Claude and Amanda this is all a big mistake, then the three of us can convince Lexa, and we'll all go down and convince the police. Yeah, right.

CK walked up to the front porch and rang the doorbell several times, but no one answered. He went back over to the window and saw the two people still sitting on the loveseat.

"Hello?" He banged on the windowpane. "Mr. and Mrs. Rhodes?"

The two figures remained motionless on the loveseat. CK tried the door handle and found it unlocked.

He opened the door and entered the house, focusing on the backs of the heads of the people on the loveseat.

"Mr. and Mrs. Rhodes?" The two on the loveseat still made no reply. CK approached the back of the loveseat. "Mr. and Mrs. Rhodes, are you all right?" He walked around to the front of the loveseat and faced the lifeless bodies of Amanda and Claude Rhodes sitting hand in hand. He gasped when he realized that someone had severed their heads and then switched them, putting Claude's head on

Amanda's body, and Amanda's head on Claude's body. CK backed away, running wildly through the house. "Lexa! Lexa, where are you?"

He ran up the staircase screaming, "Lexa! Lexa!"

He burst into Lexa's bedroom and searched it from corner to corner. A laptop displaying her Roommates homepage caught his eye. He saw the cursor resting on the journal icon, clicked it, and a table of contents menu appeared. He selected "LAST ENTRY." The display on the computer screen changed to a virtual journal page and he read it.

Cross wants to have one last session—for closure. He wants to have it at Mom and Dad's old cabin out at Lake Arrowhead, and he wants Alex to come with us. How apropos that this all ends at a place called Twin Peaks, California. Ha ha...

"Fuck!" CK picked up the phone and dialed 911.

"Nine-one-one, what's your emergency?"

CK paused for a moment, then hung up the phone. He glanced at a picture of Lexa on the desk.

I love you, Lexa Rhodes.

He ran back downstairs and frantically searched until he found Mr. and Mrs. Rhodes' address book. "Keys..." CK frantically scoured the room for the keys to Claude's car. After a half hour of fruitless searching, he spotted a wooden key rack hanging on the wall of the entryway. He raced over to the rack, but the hook labeled "Car Keys" was empty.

Damn!

He shut his eyes in defeat. When he opened them again they were intuitively drawn to the loveseat upon which Claude and Amanda sat together in death.

Oh God, I don't think I can do this.

He paced in the entryway. After a few stress-riddled minutes, he gulped a couple of deep breaths and took the first of several spine-chilling steps he must make to reach his target.

With his eyes remaining on the floor, CK stepped around in front of the loveseat and knelt between the desecrated corpses, sliding his hand into one of Claude's front pants pockets. As he dug around inside the pocket, he accidentally shifted the body and rocked Amanda's head, which was precariously perched atop Claude's neck.

Please God, please don't let me knock his—I mean her, head off.

After finding the pocket empty, he carefully removed his hand and slid it into the other front pocket until it touched something metal.

Thank you, God!

He pulled Claude's car keys from out of the dead man's pocket, jumped up, and rushed out the front door.

CHAPTER TWENTY-EIGHT

ENDGAME

Speeding down the highway, CK nervously checked the rearview mirror.

What am I doing? The killer's already been to her house and killed her aunt and uncle. I gotta tell her. I gotta warn her. But will she listen, or just run away from me? What if the killer's up there right now? Will I be able to stop him, or will I be killed too?

CK grabbed his cell phone, took out Styles's card, and dialed the number.

"Homicide."

CK exhaled. "Get me Captain Styles."

***

Sitting at her desk, Captain Styles was staring at CK's picture. "I must admit, Mr. Kane. You don't

209

give the impression of being a bloodthirsty maniac. But then what do I know? I'm just some dumbassed cop."

Excited, Lieutenant Sternn rushed toward his captain. "Cap, it's him! On the phone!" he whisper-shouted.

Styles looked up from the picture. "Him?"

"Kane!" he hissed. "On line three!"

Styles's eyes opened wide and she dropped the stack of papers she was holding. Her vision narrowed on one of the landline phones sitting on her desk. "Is the call being traced?" she asked. Sternn nodded. Styles pressed the button for line number three and picked up the receiver.

"This is Styles."

"Captain Styles, this is CK."

"Hello, CK, what can I do for you today?" She motioned for Lieutenant Sternn to pick up the other phone on her desk and listen in, which he promptly did.

"I've been to Lexa's house."

"Have you now?" Styles cupped her hand over her mouthpiece and whispered to Sternn, "Get a couple of units over there *stat*." She removed her hand from her phone and prodded, "So did you talk to her?"

"No, she's not there. And her aunt and uncle are dead. Murdered."

"I see." Styles gritted her teeth. "Did they do something to make you angry?"

"Don't jack me off, Styles!" yelled CK. *"I haven't killed anybody!"*

"Really?"

"Really. All I want is to make sure Lexa's safe. That's all, I swear to God."

"If that's really true, CK," Styles said soothingly, "why don't you come on down to the station so we can sit down and try to figure all of this out? Or if you want, you can tell me where you are and I can have a unit pick you up and bring you straight over here. What do you think? Lexa is probably counting on your help right this minute."

"I know. That's why I'm not gonna tell you to go fuck yourself, Styles. Now listen to me, and listen good. I think that the real killer is after Lexa, and I think I might know where they're headed."

"You do? Then tell me, CK, where do you think they're going?"

"I'll let you know later. I'm on my way there right now, and I have the feeling I'm gonna need your help after I get there."

"C'mon, CK, use your head. How am I supposed to come and help if you won't tell me where you're going?"

"I'm not a moron, Captain. I don't want to get there and find myself surrounded by the local police force. When I get there, I'll dial the number on the card you gave us and leave the line open for you to trace."

"Hold on a minute, CK. You should take a moment to think this through."

"Sorry, but this conversation's over." CK hung up and tossed his phone onto the passenger's seat.

"CK? CK!" Styles closed her eyes and hung up the phone. After a lingering moment, she opened her eyes and turned them toward the anxiously awaiting Lieutenant Sternn. "Let's go."

***

After what seemed an eternity, CK spotted a sign up ahead that read **'Welcome to Twin Peaks.'** Several miles beyond the sign was a private road that led into the woods. At the entrance to the road was an old, beat-up mailbox with *Rhodes* on the side of it.

CK turned onto the road, which ended about a mile down and opened up into an oval parking area surrounded by densely packed woods. A late model sedan sat parked near a dirt path. CK pulled up behind the sedan, retrieved his cellphone, and hopped out of the car. He felt the hood of the sedan. Still warm. He dialed Styles's private contact number.

"This is Styles."

After she answered, CK left his phone on and placed it atop the sedan's hood, taking off into the thick woods.

***

A deserted, burnt-out cabin sat in the middle of a barren clearing. The picturesque landscape was disfigured by the scorched ruins occupying its center.

Inside the derelict cabin, Dr. Cross sat Lexa on top of the charred dining room table.

"I'm glad you and your brother agreed to this

final session," he said, walking to the other side of the room for his medical bag. "I believe it will give you the closure you've been searching for all these years."

"Lexa," Alex whispered, "maybe this is a fucking mistake. Let's just get outta here. He can't help you anymore."

"But Alex, it's just one more session," Lexa argued. "Let's just get it over with and move on."

Sneaking a peek at Lexa, Dr. Cross removed a syringe and a bottle from his bag.

***

CK stumbled upon a path that forked in two directions. He looked back and forth, then took the path on the left.

***

Dr. Cross walked back across the room with his hands behind him.

Without taking his eyes off Cross, Alex moved closer to his twin sister and whispered into her ear, "Lexa, you've got to trust me now like when you trusted me in CK's apartment. Please, for both our sakes, let's leave now while we both still can."

"But Dr. Cross—"

"Is a sick fuck," Alex spat. "He's a manipulating perverted liar. I didn't want you to have to know about this part of it, but it's true."

Lexa felt the familiar nausea-filled twinge in her

stomach. "Okay, Alex, we'll leave."

"And go where, Lexa?" Dr. Cross questioned.

"Um…no, I, uh…"

"It's okay," Dr. Cross assured her. "Tell me."

Lexa saw Alex shaking his head with urgency, a critical warning for her to terminate her discourse with Cross. "Alex doesn't think I should be here."

"I know. Would you like to know why Alex doesn't want you here?"

Alex clenched his fists and yelled to Cross, "You swore, you fuck. You swore you'd never—"

Lexa flinched when Dr. Cross injected her arm with the syringe.

Alex lunged forward and froze when Cross raised a scalpel to Lexa's neck.

Cross's unhinged leer wantonly assaulted Lexa's drooping eyes. "You deserve to know the truth…before I kill you."

***

CK continued along the path. He sniffed the air and grimaced as he made his way through the woods.

What's that smell? What is it? It's upwind, and it's strong.

***

Lexa struggled to remain upright, sitting between her scalpel wielding doctor and her on-the-verge-of-a-meltdown twin brother.

Cross moved his face close to Lexa's right ear, deeply inhaling the scent of her perspiring skin. "You want to know a secret? Alex knows, but he'd never tell you. Those pills you've been taking all these years, they weren't for headaches."

"Don't listen to him, Sis," Alex pleaded in his sister's left ear.

Struggling to remain conscious, Lexa also struggled to understand what was being said to her. "What…? Pills? What they're for…"

Cross used his scalpel to shush Lexa's lips. "Their real purpose was to keep you from remembering certain things. Certain bad things, like what happened here the day your parents died."

"Don't listen to him, he's insane!" Alex pleaded.

"You see, my dear, your headaches were a result of your brain trying to remember. We can't have any more of that." Dr. Cross took out another syringe. "It might uncover some… unprofessionalism on my part."

Alex's eyes spewed pure hatred at Dr. Cross. "If you touch her, I'll kill you. I'll fucking kill you!"

"I'm sure Alex thinks this will do you harm," Dr. Cross said, tapping the syringe. "Alex never did trust me, not even at the age of seven when we first started our sessions."

"Shut your goddamn mouth!" Alex shouted.

"Yes, Lexa. Yet another skeleton in that big closet of yours. Well, your family's closet anyway. You see, your parents thought you'd be better off not knowing about Alex's…problems." Dr. Cross lifted the syringe. "In any case, this will help you remember something that happened a long, long time ago."

Hardly able to contain himself, Alex screamed, "I swear I'll kill you!"

"Hold still now." Dr. Cross injected Lexa.

"No! Lexa! *Lexa...*" Alex's shouting started to fade. Dr. Cross removed the needle and moved up close again to Lexa's ear.

"Clear your mind, Lexa. The only voice you'll hear is mine. The only voice you'll respond to is mine. Is that understood?"

Lexa nodded. "Yes, doctor..."

***

CK stumbled upon a lonely clearing and saw a man waist-deep inside a pit.

"What the fucking hell?" He ran to the pit and found Bastian hanging by his wrists. Empty water bottles and drums marked "LYE" lay strewn about.

"My God. Bastian." CK's eyes followed the rope up from Bastian's hands, over a branch, and down to a large rock where the end of the rope was anchored.

CK ran over to the rock. "Hold on, Bastian!" After working wildly on the huge knot, he managed to untie it, gripped the rope, and pulled with all his might.

Bastian's body slid upward painstakingly slowly. As his feet cleared the lye pit, his face contorted, the flesh below his waist pulling down and away from his torso back into the pit. The horrific sight weakened CK's grip on the rope. Bastian cried out as the rest of his dermis and muscles slid down into the lye pit. His intestines ruptured, spurting where they dangled from his midriff. Struggling to hold on to the rope, CK dropped to the ground and retched. After steadying himself, he pushed backward and tied the rope back around the rock. Through reddened and tear-filled eyes, he looked at Bastian with utter helplessness.

***

To Lexa's bewilderment, Alex stood in docile silence while Dr. Cross caressed her cheek, running his finger across Lexa's lips.

"Lexa?" he called.

Lexa weakly answered, "Yes?"

"I want you to remember when you and Alex were eight. Do you remember?"

"Yes. I remember…"

"Good girl. Now think back to the last time your parents brought you and Alex here. Think back to the day of the big fire. Think back…"

***

Eight-year-old Lexa and Alex run about carefree, having pure and natural fun as only children can. Sadly, the loud voices from within the cabin rise up and cut short their bliss-filled frolic.

"Is Daddy yelling at Mommy again?" Lexa asks her brother.

Alex nods, then takes her hand and leads her quietly inside.

Behind the closed door of their bedroom, Carl and Lisa screamed at each other.

"That settles it!" Carl shouts. "We're getting a fucking divorce!"

"Well it's about goddamn time!" Lisa yells back.

"You don't have to worry about a long, drawn-out court battle. I'll live here, and you and the kids can have the house. It'd be worth it not to have to see your goddamn face again."

"Oh no, you're not sticking me with both of them."

"Okay, fine. We'll split the deck. You'll take one and I'll take one."

The twins hug each other tightly. Alex strokes Lexa's head and leaves her sitting on the floor with her doll. He enters the garage and finds a five-gallon gas can.

Don't worry, Lexa, no one will ever separate us. Ever.

Alex splashes gasoline against the back of the cabin and underneath the window of the master bedroom. Then he enters the house and takes a pack of matches from the kitchen drawer. He passes Lexa and heads into the hallway leading to the bedrooms.

When Lexa starts to get up and follow, her brother shushes her and motions for her to sit back down.

Alex enters the hallway, soaks the floor with gasoline, then strikes a match. When he turns around, Lexa is walking into the hallway entrance. With his eyes fixed upon his twin sister's, Alex drops the match. Lexa screams when the hallway bursts into flames.

Carl opens the bedroom door, then slams it shut and he and Lisa run to the bedroom window. Alex runs out of the house and ignites the gasoline behind the cabin. Flames erupt immediately, blocking Carl and Lisa's escape.

Alex enters the house and finds Lexa near the hallway screaming through the orange flames for her parents. Carl and Lisa scream in agony from inside the burning bedroom. When Lexa turns around and sees Alex, she attacks him.

"You're killing Mommy and Daddy!" she screams. "You're killing them!"

Alex grips her by the arms. "I have to, Lexa. They were gonna split us up."

"I hate you, Alex. I hate you!"

***

Lexa squirmed upon the table and violently shook her head while screaming, "I hate you! I hate you!"

***

CK wiped the tears from his eyes when Bastian lifted up his head and begged, "Please. Please…"

CK moved closer to his friend.

"Ki…kill me, CK. Please…"

CK wept through Bastian's desperate plea. After a few agonizing moments, he made up his mind to show his friend mercy. He saw a large stone beside one of the trees, retrieved it, and lugged it over to the pit. He took a last look into his friend's eyes.

"Goodbye, Bastian."

CK hefted the stone up and slammed it against Bastian's head. He kept slamming until blood and chunks of brain oozed from his friend's shattered skull.

After the last bit of life left Bastian's body, CK dropped the stone and staggered toward the fork in the road.

***

Lexa lay semi-conscious upon the table while Dr. Cross hovered over her. She locked eyes with Alex and pleaded, "Alex…Alex, help me."

Dr. Cross glanced over to where Lexa was staring and laughed. "Alex cannot help you my dear. He's dead."

"No, he's right there."

"No, my dear, Alex exists only in your mind."

Lexa felt something physically snap in her mind. *He's right there…*

***

Eight-year-old Lexa sits alone and weeping when several rescue vehicles arrive at the burning cabin.

Tear down the wall, Lexa. Remember.

Sometime afterward, the paramedics carry three covered bodies from the burnt cabin.

Three bodies…

FRIENDS LIST

***

Lexa stared achingly at Alex.

Alex took his sister by the hand and smiled.

Lexa's mind felt like it was about to rip in half.

No, it can't be true. It's some kind of hypnotic trick or something. It has to be.

"No, you're lying. Tell him, Alex. Tell him he's lying."

Alex gazed down at Lexa and said, "No, he's not."

"I wanted you for myself," Dr. Cross said. "And I had you, to study and enjoy, so long as the pills kept your childhood memories dormant, and so long as Alex, how shall I say, stayed willing to compromise."

Lexa glared up at Cross through the blinding pain behind her eyes. "You fucking bastard."

"Yes, I'll give you that, but now to business. Apparently, the stress of the Thanksgiving trip was too much for the both of you." Cross sighed. "It's a pity. I'm really going to miss our special sessions. Oh, but you don't remember those, do you?"

A burst of anger sparked life back into Alex when Dr. Cross slid his hand up Lexa's inner thigh.

"You only have Alex to blame," Cross said. "He refused to listen to me anymore. He wanted to take over and run this show, and he almost did." He rubbed his crotch with his free hand and started to breathe heavily. "I had to put a stop to that. His agenda might have eventually led the authorities to me." Cross unbuttoned his shirt, unzipped his pants, and dropped them down around his ankles.

221

Alex's increasing rage approached critical mass, like a ripe volcano mere moments away from eruption.

"When the police find you with your wrists slashed and a scalpel in your hand, they'll simply put two and two together," explained Cross. He took a folded piece of paper out of his pocket and set it down between Lexa's legs. "If not, they'll have your typewritten confession…" He held up the scalpel and gripped Lexa's right arm at the wrist, "…and I'll be in the clear." The expression of remorse tinged Cross's face for a fleeting moment. "It is a pity about your friends, and Claude and Amanda. But, and forgive the crude analogy, a dog can't serve two masters."

When Lexa looked at Alex, he slowly dissolved before her eyes.

Cross cast his lecherous gaze upon Lexa, licked his lips, and placed the scalpel against her wrist. "And obsession is a jealous master."

Lexa's eyes shot wide open as she shouted with Alex's voice, "Leave her alone!" She reached up and grabbed Dr. Cross's forearms. "I said leave her alone!"

***

CK ran out from the woods into the clearing, where the Rhodes' derelict cabin sat like some obscure carcass laying on an ocean of green. Panting and soaked with sweat, he hurried over to one of the cabin's broken windows, peeked inside, and saw Dr. Cross struggling with Lexa. He swiped an old plank leaning against the side of the cabin and charged through the front door.

Like a man possessed, CK rushed through the cabin and swung the plank, hitting Cross square in the face.

Cross staggered backward and fell to the floor.

CK ran over to Lexa. His eyes bursting with love, he asked, "Are you all right?"

"Don't waste time with her!" Lexa shouted with Alex's voice. "Go ahead and finish the fucker!"

A bewildered CK took a couple of steps backward. What the fuck was wrong with her voice?

Lexa pointed to the jagged edge of the broken plank, and then pointed at Dr. Cross lying on the floor with blood spurting from his mouth and nose. Again with Alex's voice, she shouted, "Finish the fucker!"

CK picked up the plank and raised it over his head, standing over Dr. Cross.

Without the slightest bit of warning, Dr. Cross suddenly sat up and plunged the scalpel into CK's upper thigh, dragging the scalpel down the length of his leg until he reached the knee.

CK screamed in agony and fell to the floor.

Using pure adrenaline to counteract Cross's injections, Lexa hopped off the table and staggered toward the door. She threw it open and fled the cabin, with Dr. Cross closely giving chase.

She ran blindly through the brush. After several minutes of directionless flight, she stumbled across the parking area, ran up to Dr. Cross's car, and peered through the window at an empty ignition switch.

"Fuck!"

She spun around toward her uncle's car parked behind Cross's, but before she could check inside, she heard someone moving noisily through the brush. She crouched down next to the car and hid.

Dr. Cross ran out of the brush. After meticulously probing the surrounding area, he called out, "There's nowhere to run, Miss Rhodes." He carefully listened for any sound that might give away the whereabouts of his prey. "We can't run away from ourselves—our true selves. Good or evil, right or wrong, sane or insane, we are what we are."

While crouched and hidden from sight, Lexa started drawing upon every newly awakened memory of her years of rape and molestation from Cross. The rage in her head all at once spewed forth like boiling water from a covered pot.

Lexa stood straight up and shouted, "Yes, doctor, we are!" With madness in her eyes, she rushed full speed toward Dr. Cross. When she neared him, he stood his ground and struck out at her with his scalpel. To the doctor's surprise, Lexa slid down between Cross's legs and swept him off his feet with her arms. He fell face first on the ground and released the scalpel.

Lexa sneered.

You're dead, Dr. Cross.

She grabbed the scalpel, rolling Cross onto his back and straddling him. "It's like Alex always says…" She held the scalpel to his neck and grinned. "Never start what you can't finish." Without a second thought, Lexa sliced Dr. Cross's throat. Arterial spray covered her as she cut deeper and deeper. Cross gurgled blood and viscera, reached toward Lexa, and breathed his last breath.

***

Captain Styles sped into the parking area, slammed on the brakes, and jumped out with her gun drawn. Lieutenant Sternn hopped out from the passenger's side and followed his captain's lead. After scanning the area, Styles ran over to Lexa. "Are you all right?"

Lexa nodded.

Styles glanced down at Dr. Cross's dead body. "Where's CK?"

Lexa pointed toward the trail that led to the cabin. "He saved my life."

"CK saved your life?"

"Yes," Lexa said. "I'd be dead if it wasn't for him."

"Stay here, I'll be right back." Weapon in hand, Captain Styles raced for the cabin with her lieutenant in tow.

Moments after Styles and Sternn disappeared into the woods, Alex comes out of the woods and approaches his twin sister. He and Lexa lovingly embrace.

Without breaking her hug, Lexa says, "You saved me."

"No, *we* saved *us*."

"I love you, Alex."

"I love you, Lexa. And I promise, we'll be together forever."

"Forever isn't long enough." A veil of sadness covers Lexa's face when she breaks their hug and faces Alex.

"What's the matter?"

"You're dead. How can we be together?"

Alex whispers into Lexa's ear. When he finishes, his sister smiles widely.

"Always?" Lexa takes Alex's right hand and places it over her heart.

"Always…" Alex repeats. "Forever?" Alex brings up Lexa's right hand and places it over his heart.

"Forever."

The tears raining down Lexa's face recede as she falls into her brother's eyes…

***

Captain Styles and Lieutenant Sternn helped CK limp out of the cabin. When they exited the woods, they saw Lexa wrap her arms around herself and wave goodbye.

CHAPTER TWENTY-NINE

CASE CLOSED

Three Months Later

Captain Styles carried a box full of files into the Long Beach Police Station's evidence room. She placed it on a shelf filled with similar boxes and wrote "Case Closed" on the label. Lieutenant Sternn entered the room carrying a large, heavy footlocker.

"New lunchbox, Sternn?" Styles joked.

Sternn laughed. "Ever hear of workplace harassment, Captain?" He set the footlocker down with a huff at Captain Styles's feet. "The impound guys were giving Cross's boat a final inspection when they found this hidden below deck." He wiped the sweat off his brow and plopped down on top of the footlocker. "Boy am I glad this case is over, Cap. I wouldn't be able to sleep at night knowing that psychopath was still out there on the loose somewhere. That was one seriously sick fucking guy."

"Have you opened it yet?" Styles asked.

"Opened what yet?"

"The big thing under your big ass."

"Nope. I thought I'd save that pleasure for you, seeing as how involved you were with this case." Sternn took a large screwdriver out of his pocket and broke the padlock on the locker. "*Bon appétit, Mon Capitan.*" The lieutenant left the room.

Captain Styles opened the footlocker. She flipped through various pediatric medical records, psychological evalutions, and explicit photographs of Lexa as a child. Her expression changed from one of curiosity to that of dread. Styles became faint and plopped down to the floor. "Oh my God…"

CHAPTER THIRTY

TILL DEATH DO US PART

CK carried his blushing bride, Lexa Kane, over the threshold of the Hotel Maya's honeymoon suite. He kicked the door closed, set her down, and adjusted the brace on his right leg.

"Check it out," he said, pointing up to the mirrored ceiling above the bed.

Lexa giggled and kissed CK, long and passionately. "Now aren't you glad we waited? Well, you're about to be well rewarded for your patience, sir."

Lexa took CK's hand and led him to the bedroom where she threw her purse on the bed next to the pillows. She embraced CK, and kissed him wantonly.

She pushed him away, undressed down to her bridal lingerie and laid back on the bed. She moved her purse toward the headboard whilst stretching seductively across the mattress.

After feasting his eyes on the irresistible sight

posed in front of him, CK stripped off his clothes and climbed on the bed next to his new wife. Lexa giggled, pulled CK toward her, and kissed him. As their passion intensified, CK moved his hand down and caressed Lexa's inner thigh. She responded with hushed sounds of pleasure.

When he moved his hand up her thigh, Lexa stopped him, "Oh God. I'm sorry, I just…"

CK shushed Lexa. "Don't be afraid. You can trust me."

"Okay." Lexa let go and resumed kissing her new husband. As their passion mounted, CK's hand moved upward toward his wife's genitals. Lexa moaned softly, moving her hands toward the headboard.

CK's hand stopped and he yanked it away from Lexa with the visage of abject disgust. "What the fuck?"

Struggling to wrap his mind around what was happening, he stared at his bride through eyes laden with bewildered disenchantment. "How could…how could you…"

Tears rolling down Lexa's cheeks, she pulls a large hunting knife from her purse and plunges it into her husband's abdomen. CK cried out in agony and fell back onto the bed.

Lexa jumps on top of him and stabs him wildly and repeatedly while desperately pleading, "Love me! Love me! Love me!"

The mad carnage intensifies, and a warped conversation starts up inside Lexa's irreparably damaged psyche, one which takes place inside the hooded figure's filthy, dimly lit room which is slowly starting to engulf in flames–the room being the mental construct where Alex's psyche resides...Alex's *hooded* psyche.

Alex: I told you he wasn't the one.

Lexa: I guess you were right.

Alex: I'm always right when it comes to us.

***

In the cabin's master bedroom, Carl and Lisa Rhodes desperately cower from the flames.

Alex: Mom and Dad made a terrible mistake. They shouldn't have ever tried to divide us.

Eight-year-old Lexa struggles with Alex as the cabin burns around them.

Alex: They didn't understand, we're indivisible.

Lexa runs out of the cabin as it starts to collapse.

Alex: You didn't understand back then either...

Eight-year-old Alex snatches up his father's hunting knife and chases after Lexa.

Back in the present, Lexa is still viciously stabbing CK and shouting incoherently...

Alex tackles Lexa, viciously stabbing her to death as light from the blazing fire merges their shadows on the clearing's floor.

Alex: So I had to send you away.

Alex gazes into Lexa's lifeless eyes. He let go of the knife and grieved his loss.

Alex: And then bring you back.

Alex took off his clothes, then undressed Lexa and put on her clothes. He wrapped his hair into a ponytail and tied it with his sister's ribbon.

Alex: My love for you brought you back.

Alex picked up Lexa's body and threw it into the burning cabin.

Alex: You were reborn and we were together again.

Alex wept as several rescue vehicles arrived at the burning cabin.

Moaning, Lexa continues plunging the knife into CK…

***

Behind the closed doors of his home office, Dr. Cross talked with eight-year-old Alex/Lexa.

Alex: But Cross, that fuck. When he found out the truth about us, he said he'd tell the police unless I let him…have his way.

Dr. Cross prepared photographic equipment during one of Alex/Lexa's sessions.

Alex: So I had to protect you. I couldn't let you know about the special sessions.

Dr. Cross undressed young Alex/Lexa and then undressed himself.

Alex: I'd put you to sleep and let the perverted fuck have his way with me.

Dr. Cross moved toward Alex/Lexa.

Lexa: I'm so sorry you had to go through all of that for me.

Alex: I'd gladly burn in Hell for you.

Unhinged and drenched in blood, Lexa slices and

carves into her lifeless husband's neck.

Inside the darkened student apartment, hooded Alex/Lexa cut into Kimber's neck.
Lexa: I'm still sad for Kimber and the others.

At the Thanksgiving feast, hooded Alex/Lexa put Kimber's head in a boiling stock pot.
Alex: You were letting them come between us, so I had to get rid of them.

***

On the Queensbay Bridge, hooded Alex/Lexa place a noose around Paige's neck.
Lexa: I'm sorry I allowed that. It'll never happen again.

Hooded Alex/Lexa take pictures while watching Palmer burn to death in the Jacuzzi.
Alex: I know it won't.

Hooded Alex/Lexa carve on Cassie as she lay screaming against her apartment's door.
Alex: And with Claude and Amanda out of the picture, there's no one left to keep us apart.

Hooded Alex/Lexa enter CK's bedroom, plug an SD card into CK's desktop, and upload pictures of the murders.
Alex: Now we are one.

While sitting under the St. Vincent Thomas

Bridge, hooded Alex/Lexa render Bastian unconscious with a stun gun.

Lexa: Now we are one.

Hooded Alex/Lexa attack Amanda and Claude in the living room.

Alex/Lexa: Now we are one.

Soaked in blood, Lexa stares up at the mirrored ceiling and smiles. Her cleaved reflection, one half Lexa's face and the other half Alex's face, smiles back down at her.

***

The honeymoon suite doorbell rings. Lexa, now cleaned up and dressed in fresh white sexy bridal lingerie, approaches the door. She opens it to find Senator Storm standing in the hallway holding several wrapped gifts.

"Senator Storm! What a nice, unexpected surprise."

Storm tried, but failed, to keep his eyes and other parts from bulging as he gave Lexa a quick onceover. After a few moments of wanton lust, he regained his power of speech.

"Congratulations, my dear. I'm sorry I missed the ceremony, but I was unavoidably detained."

"No worries, Senator. I understand," she simpers coyly, whispering sweet nothings to Storm with her eyes.

Storm loosened his tie. "I'm sorry for this intrusion, but I wanted to drop these off before my flight back to the capitol."

"Oh, how thoughtful of you."

Storm stood speechless while Lexa gave him all the right signals. "Well…I'll just leave these with you."

Lexa gazes deeply into Storm's eyes. "Why don't you come in for a moment, Senator?"

After his brain took a moment to process the implications of the invitation, Storm glanced around nervously. "Are you sure CK won't mind?"

"Oh no, he won't mind. Besides…" Lexa reaches out and plays with Storm's tie, "…the more the merrier."

She flashes a sexy smile and gives Storm a come-hither wink.

Storm gave her a lascivious onceover and eagerly entered the suite.

Lexa grins and closes the door.

THE END

ACKNOWLEDGEMENTS

I would like to express my deep and loving gratitude to Robert Watson, Sr. (Dad), Edwene Watson (Mom), and Eulalie Smyer (LaLa), three of the strongest, most loving people I've ever known, and for whom I owe my life. My wife Lori for all her unpaid hours of proofreading and encouragement; my son Robby, my "right hand," whose help and support allowed me the time and opportunity to write; and my ten-year-old son Mark for his wonderful, loving personality that keeps me moving forward no matter what obstacles cross my path.

I would like to offer a deep and sincere thanks to my high school AP English teacher James Cross, the only teacher who showed that he cared, and the only teacher I care to remember. It was his passion for literature and tireless expectation of excellence from his students that fanned the authorial flame inside me, a flame of potential that he took the time to recognize and embolden. Thank you, Mr. Cross.

Thanks to everyone at Limitless Publishing, and a special thanks to Felicia A. Sullivan—editor extraordinaire!

Also, thanks to Remy, TL, BK, DK, SB, FB, PC, SW, JB, Dottie, Dina, and Joslyn.

ABOUT THE AUTHOR

Rob Watson was born in Santa Monica, California. He is married and is the father of three children. He is the owner of Damaged Psyche Productions. He is a horror/sci-fi fanatic and has been ever since early childhood. He has been imagining and writing stories for as far back as he can remember. Some of his idols are Rod Serling, Steven King, David Cronenberg, Edgar Allan Poe, Alfred Hitchcock, Wes Craven, and Dan Curtis. Rob studied film and creative writing at Long Beach City College and California State University, Long Beach, after which he spent a couple of years working on movie production crews (as set PA, second assistant director, boom, etc.). Since then, he has written almost a dozen feature length screenplays (mostly horror and/or sci-fi) as well as numerous short stories and scripts. He has two original screenplays currently in pre-production and has written several "work-for-hire" scripts.

My website:
Damaged Psyche Productions
www.damagedpsycheproductions.com/

Amazon author page:
http://www.amazon.com/-/e/B01GITH0G8

Goodreads author page:
https://www.goodreads.com/author/dashboard

Facebook: *Rob Watson*
https://www.facebook.com/profile.php?id=10001
0542909132&fref=photo

Twitter: *DamagedPsyche1*
https://twitter.com/DamagedPsyche1?lang=en

Wattpad: *@RobWatson13*
https://www.wattpad.com/user/RobWatson13

Instagram: *robwatson.dpp*
https://www.instagram.com/robwatson.dpp/

IMDB link: *Rob Watson (IX)*
http://www.imdb.com/name/nm7789883/?ref_=tt
_ov_wr

Author Central Information:
amazon.com/author/robwatson